Amphibians

Also by the Author

Off Island
A Thousand and One Nights

Amphibians

Lara Tupper

Stories

Leapfrog Press
New York and London

Published in 2021 in the United States by
Leapfrog Press LLC

www.leapfrogpress.com

Distributed in the United States by
Consortium Book Sales and Distribution
St. Paul, Minnesota 55114
www.cbsd.com

Author photo by © Elaina Mortali

First Edition

ISBN 978-1-948585-12-5

Library of Congress Cataloging-in-Publication Data

Printed and bound by CPI Group (UK) Ltd., Croydon CR0 4YY

 The Forest Stewardship Council® is an international non-governmental organisation that promotes environmentally appropriate, socially beneficial, and economically viable management of the world's forests. To learn more visit www.fsc.org

For Bobby, my love

"The amphibian is only ever as warm as the day."
—*Extreme Baby Animals*
(National Geographic film)

Contents

Amphibians

On the lake the loons are sparse, but Helen has acquired a throw pillow, a present from the girl, stitched by a local artisan and bought with allowance money from an overpriced gift shop. There is logic in the pillow's central loon—its black curve of neck, the red border seamed from interlocking triangles. It has become Helen's necessary possession in the vast barn that is their Maine summer home. The central stone chimney is cold until mid-September and here Helen leans with the pillow just so, soft between her spine and the quarried bits that are the fireplace.

The chimney bench perch is hers. No one questions this. There she can sit in the quiet and not see actual loons. She can see black trees backlit by sun, the muzzy water, the airplane skeleton, her large husband and the thin carpenter pausing to gather tools on the dock. She sees the former Congressman, his shirttails still tucked, hands on hips in irritation, as far from the working men as is permissible without appearing rude. She sees the girl, not her own, swimming far. From the bench they are actors Helen can direct and the wine makes this thought important.

Amphibians

Today the marred oak table holds her glass, a month-old *New Yorker,* watercolor greeting cards, blank inside, and a leaky calligraphy pen that plumes against her finger pads. Someone they don't know well has died in a car crash and she must send a note about it today, tomorrow at the latest.

Helen eats the cheese, which has been sitting out long enough. The tangy rot of it in her mouth becomes a memory of hitchhiking in an orange miniskirt with the girl's mother. It was the summer after their junior year and the skirt tugged on Helen's shapely ass. She'd known it was shapely. The girl's mother wore a miniskirt too, a different shade. They'd shared a bag of bread and cheese, walking slowly on a gold Tuscan road, dipping in hands to tear. Gouda lodged under their fingernails. They were waiting for men to take them places and this happened. They met brothers and took off their skirts for them, separately, in hostel rooms so dirty Helen hadn't wanted to step on the floor, not even in stockings. She'd thought she was pregnant. But August came and they landed at JFK and she began to bleed the next day, as though her nether regions had just been waiting to make it back home.

Helen had told this story to the girl, who perhaps hadn't realized there was life before she was born. Or that her mother hadn't always been like this, braced for the girl's attention. They'd seen vast olive orchards, eaten poorly, fornicated with men who were not their husbands. It was important for the girl to know.

Helen knocks her gold ring, hazelnut-sized, against the lip of the glass, a perfect angle of sound breaking the silence. She quits the watercolor card, allows the next true, steady thought to blare through, which is, *Who fucking cares?* She means the men, the inert plane, the girl making ripples with small arms. The temperature of the cheese makes no difference, certainly not to the girl, already locked in some private battle with herself.

But in they'll come with grubby fingers and Helen will allow it. She'll adopt the posture of generosity, allow for the cessation of their hunger. She'll gesture to the pile of plumped, brown towels, dried often but rarely washed. They don't ask, so they'll never have to know.

·   ·   ·   ·

The girl can swim far, which scares her father. She likes the immersion, her limbs easing through. While floating and watching tips of pines, it's possible to imagine she's not human at all. The water in her ears is how she hears things. Buoyancy is all she's permitted to feel. She can envision a different kind of existence, one where swimming is required to survive.

At school there's a boy who believes the girl is responsible for Jesus' death. He boasts about his father's anti-Semitic tattoo and, when he's captain, he picks her last for teams. She's interested in this boy because of his serious eyes and because he runs faster than anyone else in gym.

The girl knows she's responsible for the shifts in volume and temperature in her parents' house and assumes it's the same on the lake. It's not always unpleasant. She's an experiment, a source of interest. The spotlight beams down, microscopic cells smooshed between glass slides. No one knows what she is or how she'll turn out.

The girl's father yells from the dock. He's not kidding this time.

She'll have to explain again—the survival gene in her DNA— she won't go under. She can live where others can't, because of her adaptation.

It's only after she returns, heaving herself onto the dock without the use of the ladder, that she feels human again. The drips from her limbs spread out into wetness, the boards changing color because of her efforts. Her lungs are working, her shoulders ache. It's the best sensation she knows so far, this after-swim tiredness. Her body used on its own accord.

Her father holds out a brown towel in his good shoes. "You don't have to swim so far. Where's your mother?"

The girl doesn't answer because they both know she's at the office still.

"Did you hear me from out there? Is it cold?" Her father likes to swim too but he hasn't brought his suit and won't borrow someone else's Speedos.

She wants to say, *The chill of the water—it doesn't last.* Most grown ups can only think about the smack of it, the dread. This is what it means to get older.

The skinny carpenter jumps in, hooting.

"Fuck!" he says. Then, "Sorry," remembering the girl.

The carpenter is always there, tall and longhaired and barefoot, so the grown ups call him JC. He's helping Ned with the amphibian, a plane that lands on water. No one wants it on the lake except Ned, JC and the girl. It will be noisy. The frame blocks the view. The epoxy drips into weeds and may kill the cattails. But they keep building. They smoke joints and laugh and try to understand the manual. (The engine was the wrong size. A wing split after a storm.) They've been at it for five years already.

The girl is not allowed to ride in the plane, ever. She doesn't argue this point because she doesn't want to fly. She wants to watch it glide on the water like a loon.

Ned stretches and lets out a long fart, which makes the girl giggle.

"Daniel," he says to her father. No one else calls him this. "No suits required."

"I suppose not," her father says in his Maine accent. His voice is throaty, dense. His smile isn't real and he doesn't move to undress.

Amphibians

Ned laughs like her father has just said something brilliant, a bellow that reminds the girl of the boy in gym. It could be an *I'm making fun of you* laugh. It's hard to tell.

At home her father laughs at Ned, at the fact that he's *paid* to listen. A shrink!

Her mother says, *Maybe the summers are his release.*

Her father says he would pay to see it, Ned sitting quietly in a chair listening for an hour.

The girl suspects she's the only one who truly likes Ned. His loudness is like a plow scooting snow into ditches. It's clear, at least. He has a roach clip and a pocket watch. He has L.L. Bean flannel shirts and many pairs of Speedos and this is all he wears in summer over his barrel belly and tiny legs. The corner of the dock dips under before he slices in but the girl doesn't laugh at him. He's a fat man and a graceful diver—it's possible to be both. He was a lifeguard once. He taught her how to breathe in the water, how to blow out bubbles from her nose by ducking under and holding onto the ladder. He taught her how to dive in stages: sit and dive, kneel and dive, stand and dive. How he'd grinned the day she got it, standing. How able she'd felt, surfacing, sturdy as a boat.

Last week, Ned tried to teach the girl how to use an ax and her father had protested.

Her father can't understand how important it is, using a tool to cut things. He doesn't fit in at the camp, with his sobriety and lack of swearing. But he's here because he's semi-retired, because he's a lot older than her mother and he never really liked practicing law anyway. He liked politics, but that was a long time ago. Now he writes letters to the editor and organizes anti-nuke meetings. There's a little machine in her parents' bedroom that measures radiation, beeping and blinking a red light whenever a speck of it is detected.

Her mother fits in at the camp, because her mother used to

hitchhike and wear miniskirts and eat cheese from a plastic bag and undress for handsome Italians.

•　　　•　　　•　　　•

On the dock with the men, the air shifts into evening. There are bugs that bite and the smell of pot. Ned offers the roach clip to her father and again he refuses. Helen builds a fire outside in the pit and the girl throws in plastic forks, watches them curl like fiddleheads. There's a hammock that's always damp where someone's butt has been. There's cheese that looks like it should be thrown out but instead the men are cooing over it, smearing it onto crackers you can't find in Maine.

There's the usual talking, debates that circle and climb and cause sparks and Ned takes the opposite side and the girl's father tries not to bite but he can't help himself, and soon he's shouting even though they all agree. Her father doesn't mention Congress, doesn't say *Kennedy, Johnson and Ford*. And because he doesn't, Ned has to make up stories that no one can quite counter. He has to make himself fatter even though he's the fattest one there.

There's no room for the girl in this kind of talking. She practices in her head but by the time she's ready they aren't talking about the same thing anymore. When she tries to slide in, they talk over her. She'll never be loud enough.

It's her own fault, she understands, for *not speaking up*, which is one of the worst sins.

The girl finds her Sony Walkman and takes the hammock seat and plays the Journey song she's memorized. There's something exciting about it, the way the drums are a force moving forward. She smells the dampness in her hair. Not quite mold. Active algae, pond scum, places good for frogs. She wants this stuff on her skin, wants to be closer to those creatures and further from the adults around the fire.

Amphibians

Without asking she borrows Helen's yellow sweatshirt, balled at her feet on the hammock. The sweatshirt smells like sour wine and garlic, which is what Manhattan smells like, the girl decides, because that's where Helen and Ned are from.

In Manhattan there are entire stores devoted to sweatshirts. You can get free pins at the counter, checkered like an old fashioned cab, and the girl has many that Helen has dropped in her palm. Helen has sweatshirts in every shade and when they get too stained with wine or cooking oil, she says the girl can keep them. The girl has her eye on a turquoise one, soft and faded with a small tear at the collar.

The cassette side ends and the girl's stomach gurgles, like there are tadpoles colliding inside. *Do you have an apple?* she could ask. But she doesn't know which Helen she's getting today, the one who seems to welcome her girl features among the men or the one who won't look at the girl directly, who speaks in a straight line, a blank teacher's voice. The girl has learned to ask questions, adults like this, but on certain days Helen's answers are hard quips. BB pellets.

Every summer Helen's hair is different—brown or red, shoulder-length or chopped. This year she has dreadlocks and everyone says she looks fantastic. Someone says it every day, which gives Helen a momentary shine.

"Great hair-do," her father tries today, during a pause in the arguing with Ned.

"Thanks, Dan," says Helen. There is calmness between them, an accord.

"Rastafari!" says Ned.

The girl's father cringes.

There are times when Ned calls Helen by her middle name, which is Abigail. He says it like she's a Duchess and he's her servant. It's their way of flirting and the girl feels better when they're like this.

Amphibians

"You're shivering," the father says to the girl and it's true, there's a jangle she's been ignoring, her lips moving on their own.

The girl tips herself from the hammock and follows Helen and the men inside but there's too much commotion to ask about the apple. Helen searches for the beautiful salad bowl, carved from a foreign tree and shiny with use. She chops the greens, complicated leaves, not iceberg. She asks the girl to help set the table and the girl feels too shy to refuse. She's getting the good Helen today. She tells the girl about her high school students, how they say "bad" when they mean good. "It's *bad*." She laughs about this, drinks her wine. She's the cool teacher who takes them on the subway to see theater. She directs the student play, never a musical. Musicals are vapid, she says, though she knows the girl has the soundtracks to *Godspell* and *A Chorus Line* and hopes to play Diana Morales someday, the "I Feel Nothing" solo.

Last summer the girl had an autograph book and Helen wrote, "To thine own self be true," in handwriting with neat, tall loops, little actors in tights.

Ned didn't want to sign it. "I can't spell."

"Not even your name?" said Helen.

He'd scribbled his name with no message.

Now Helen slices the onions evenly and Ned tells the story again, the one where he ends up in a jail in Mexico. Helen lets the girl unscrew the next bottle and the cork comes out in one piece.

"Perfection," say Ned.

She has a collection at home, red stains on lower halves.

Then JC's curvy girlfriend arrives and they leave with arms wrapped around waists. There's no separating them.

"Attached at the hip," says Ned.

They laugh, exit.

Amphibians

Finally the girl's mother arrives, pretty in a long white skirt with no slip and everyone smiles a lot as she calls out hello. The girl wants her to go swimming but it's too buggy, too cold, and instead her mother sips the wine Helen has poured. She lifts a piece of cheese, then puts it down. She tells a funny story about a crazy client and the girl's father sits close, his hand on her shoulder.

The girl wants to be sitting where the father is. She kicks at the table leg. She's cold and she asks for a different sweatshirt, a dry one.

"You know where to find them," says Helen, which means the girl has permission to go into their bedroom and snoop.

On the dresser there are film cases filled with pot and small piles of chunky jewelry, slabs of silver and gold. The bed is unmade. The TV hangs above from a thick chain, a suspended boulder that could crash and kill them both in their sleep. There are channels that show, on mute, naked people crouching and thrusting and car chases that end badly. In the closet there are rows of leather shoes that are the same. There is one black dress that is made by someone famous and will never be handed down. The girl tries it on, feeling in the dark of the closet for the door to slide behind her. She puts it back on the hanger inside out. She takes the turquoise sweatshirt.

The girl holds her belly. "Are you hungry?" says the girl's father.

"We're having steak," says Helen.

"We should go home and feed the puppy," says the girl's father.

"Daniel," says Ned. "Relax."

"I'll just finish this," says the girl's mother.

"They won't take long to cook," says Helen.

The girl's father reaches for his coat, but it's Helen's coat. He didn't have one.

19

Amphibians

"I'll be right behind," says the girl's mother. Her legs are splayed, her skirt hiked up. Her eyes shine. Her toes are the typical gnarled nubs of a former dancer. The girl can stick a pin in one callused side and her mother doesn't flinch.

The girl's father kisses the top of her mother's head, closing his eyes as his lips meet the curls. Helen watches them. She sees the sweatshirt the girl is wearing, turquoise, the tear at the collar, the splotch of ink on the sleeve.

"Keep it," says Helen. Her voice is high. She is in the far-off place where her hands flutter, where her husband is not so fat, where the two of them in the large house with the thin carpenter are enough.

"Oh, she has plenty," says the girl's father.

"I don't have turquoise," says the girl.

"Thank you," says her mother, looking at the girl.

"Thank you," says the girl's father, and steers the girl away.

In the car the girl asks what they'll have for dinner and her father says, "Not raw steak." He tunes the country music station and they sing a Willie Nelson song as the sky bleeds alien orange shades.

"Don't you ever get in car with someone who's drunk," says her father.

"I won't," says the girl. Someone has died recently, a crash on Route 27, a woman they don't know.

"Or stoned. Drunk or stoned."

It will take three more songs before they're home in the woods with no lake, which the girl is still thinking about. Now that the humans have left the dock, there will be spiders, spindly and fast, the same gray as the old boards. They'll skim the water with their perfect legs, light enough to fly along the surface.

Her father is still humming. Waylon Jennings now.

"Did Helen and Ned ever try to have a kid?" she asks, though she knows the answer.

He turns down the dial to hear her. She asks again.

"They did try. A few years ago. It didn't work out for them."

"They couldn't have a baby or they decided they didn't want one?"

"I think a little of both." He weighs his response. "Some people just aren't meant to be parents."

The girl considers this. "At least they have JC."

"Yes," says her father. "I suppose that's true."

· · · ·

When her mother comes home her hair is wet. "I went swimming!" she says, which is hard to believe.

"How come?" says the girl.

"Was it cold?" says her father. He's making pasta and an ordinary salad as the girl sets the table.

"I didn't have a suit," she says. "I had to borrow one of Helen's." But they both know it's a lie. Her skirt is damp and see-through where she didn't dry off.

"She's my oldest friend," says her mother. She wraps her thin arms around his waist.

"I know," he says. He kisses her, removes her hands, then whacks the iceberg lettuce with a blade.

At dinner her parents talk about the law office they share, her father's voice rising in annoyance at people who aren't there. Her mother laughs or doesn't laugh, or reminds him to send the bill, or asks the girl if she's still hungry—the pasta is still on her plate.

"You don't have to eat it all," her father says.

The girl knows her presence is important. They need her there to talk around and under, if not to.

They talk about Helen's hair.

"Awful," says her mother. "But. She likes it. So what's the harm?"

Amphibians

Is it awful or is there no harm? The girl's hair is the same, just longer. She needs a trim but her father doesn't want her to cut it, ever.

"It's too bad you sold the camp," says the girl to change the subject. Her parents are quiet as they chew. She knows why they sold it. There was only a tiny changing house and a muddy trail of two-by-fours. When her father stopped being in Congress, when her mother decided she wanted to be a mother, they moved back to Maine from Washington DC and found they didn't have any money. The mother thought of her college roommate first, still in Manhattan. Who wouldn't want a summer place on a lake? They'd shingled the new house together as teams, Ned and her mother against Helen and her father.

"Who won?" the girl asks. "The shingle contest?"

"We did," says her mother. "Not that it was a competition." She laughs. "We can go there anytime we want. That was part of the deal."

"I want to go swimming every day," says the girl.

Her father at the head of the table taps his glass of water with his wedding ring. He looks hard at the chiseled flecks in the glass, the way the light shines in through the liquid.

"It's my turn. I'll take you tomorrow," says her mother, her voice a decisive bell, and the girl feels relief. Tomorrow she can swim far and her father doesn't have to know.

It's nine o'clock before anyone remembers to feed the dog, who isn't allowed to go to the camp because there are nails everywhere. The girl is okay with this. She prefers to swim alone.

•   •   •   •

When the girl shows up with her mother to swim again, there are white slivers on the kitchen floor. Helen's loon pillow is blackened (snatched and tossed in the fire pit). Her eyes are swollen. It's the first time the girl has seen Helen without shadow and liner.

Ned has taken the van somewhere for the day.

"I'm sorry," says the girl. She means about the pillow, because it was something Helen liked.

The girl has started saying this a lot, *I'm sorry*, though her mother tells her not to.

"You haven't done anything wrong," her mother says now.

"I know. I'm sorry."

Her mother stays inside to talk to Helen and JC takes her down to the dock, where they sit on the old boards and JC snaps a long stick into tiny pieces. They say nothing for ages.

There's an ongoing competition, the girl understands. Each day the teams and maneuvers change—someone advances, someone retreats. It's hard to tally the results because she misses the nighttime, when all the action happens. Plates get smashed, Helen trips, the gardener isn't invited back.

As far as the girl can tell, she's the one who's winning because she doesn't have to play yet. Soon she'll be judged by whom she can quote, which opinions she can recite and how quickly. There won't be time to think, she'll have to hurl herself in, jam her foot to stop the slamming door.

"What did Ned do?" says the girl to break the quiet on the dock.

"Oh, nothing. He was being a dick," says JC.

Was it nothing or was he being a dick?

JC tells the girl that he's related to her in a complicated way, not a brother but a cousin, twice removed. Before the girl was born, when the not-brother was a teenager and didn't have anywhere else to go, her father took care of him for a while.

She has an almost-brother? Why has no one bothered to mention this before?

She remembers the time, last summer, when JC lifted her

23

like a baby and threw her in, how the shock of it made her afraid of the lake for the first time. It was supposed to be funny, but the force of being thrown made water shoot up her nose.

She'd switched it then, because she wanted to like JC. She knew how to blow water out her nose, she'd been taught, so it could have been her own fault for not reacting quickly enough.

Other than throwing her in, the not-brother is okay. He listens now on the dock as she tells him how far she can swim. He seems genuinely impressed by this. Then he goes back to the airplane hull to study the manual.

Because her father isn't there, the girl can swim to Moby Dick, the white rock across the lake. The rock is part of an island with a path through the woods, which leads to the YMCA camp on the other side.

She swims, singing show tunes in her head until she gets there. The steady breathing, the even strokes—she's a different creature now. She slides herself onto the white rock to feel her chest moving, deep and solid, her skin warm.

She follows the trail, careful where she steps. The soldiers are chasing her and she can't leave any sign. The German shepherds have her scent. She has to go fast enough to lose them but not so fast she'll break twigs or drip water from her hair. The men will shoot without thinking, just because she's half-Jewish. This is what the boy at school tells her at recess.

She's so absorbed she thinks the sounds are real soldiers. But the shouting, she hears, is actually her not-brother. He's canoed to the rock, trying to find her.

"Fuck," he says, leaning over, resting his hands on his knees like a gym teacher. He wheezes air into his smoky lungs and spits into the pine needles, orange and soft on the ground. He wears cut off jeans with the pocket flaps sticking out and no shoes. His feet are almost black. "How did you swim all that way?"

Amphibians

The girl realizes she's in a bathing suit, crosses her arms over her chest. She decides not to mention the Nazis.

"Your dad would shit a brick," he says. They stay that way, facing each other in the woods, chirrups of small birds around them, waiting for her not-brother to catch his breath. He's not as old as he seems. He has the terrified look on his face she feels so often inside and in that moment she understands it's the truth, she's related to him somehow.

He promises not to tell her father if she promises not to tell her father. "Or your mother," he adds, though they both know this isn't as crucial.

As she swims back, the canoe by her side, it's not unpleasant. She matches the pace of his paddle strokes. He smokes a cigarette, breathing in and out without using his hands, a human train. She's impressed by this and wants to try it herself someday.

Later, in the campfire circle, Helen and the plumber argue about Reagan.

Her mother says they have to go home, without mentioning the dog, and then she hugs Helen for a long time.

"Good swim?" her mother asks in the car. "I hope you didn't go out too far."

"Am I related to JC?" the girl answers.

"Oh, very distantly. Everyone's related in this town."

"But we are related somehow."

"Somehow, yes. You'll have to ask your father."

•　　　•　　　•　　　•

An accountant and his girlfriend arrive from Brooklyn. They pitch a tent and the girl sneaks in to see a tan cup like a small, loose Frisbee and gel that is not Bacitracin. *Sex,* she understands. *In a tent.*

The girl never knows who'll be there on the dock. There are

stone masons and landscapers Ned and Helen have collected, more men than women. Ned bribes them with beer and pot so they'll stay beyond 5:00 pm. He tells them to take a dip, bring their pets, and sometimes there's a dumb black lab who jumps in after rocks and a prissy collie who won't go in at all.

There are visitors from away—teachers and shrinks, a promoter for a famous rock band, a physicist. Helen has a calendar and the weekends have X's with names. Sometimes they stay longer, calling in sick. They bring food you can't find in Maine: Mallomar cookies and Hebrew National hot dogs. They bring boring magazines and hog the hammock, peering at lines and lines of words. Few of them have children.

The accountant brings a large inflatable rowboat named Das Boot, a joke the girl doesn't understand. JC jumps from the dock into the boat's center and lands perfectly, slicing the bottom with the X-Acto knife he forgot to remove from his belt. The girl cheers, until Das Boot begins to hiss, the air released.

"We can fix that," says her father. "Do you have a rubber patch?" But no one can find the little kit that came with the float. It sits there, sinking, until it's a flap of gray rubber roped to the dock. A week later, the accountant and his girlfriend and their tent long gone, JC heaves it from the lake, waterlogged, and a week after that it's dry enough to burn, which the girl can't wait to see. She helps to build the fire and imagines the plastic will curl magnificently—like a fork, folding in and disappearing— like the Wicked Witch of the West, the ugly thing gone at last.

Except that it doesn't burn. It smolders, making black smoke so noxious the Fire Marshall comes. Her father shakes the Fire Marshall's hand and apologizes before hosing it out himself.

Ned is embarrassed. The girl can see it in the set of his jaw and his silence, his whiskey glass, refilled. Her father could have leverage, could berate him at last. But her father says nothing until they're at home.

Amphibians

"Dipshit," he begins.

Her mother passes the salad.

• • • •

For her birthday, the girl gets a Speak and Spell, a giant talking calculator for words, and she beats Ned every time. He delights in this, her ability to type in "beggar" and "pontoon" before he can even acknowledge what these nouns resemble. She has found a chink in his armor and he allows her to wriggle in a little spear, not too sharp.

• • • •

Someone brings the *New York Times* list of 100 Best Books of All Time and Helen is going to read every one. The girl's mother has read a third of them already. Her father shrugs. He likes biographies and there are only two included. Ned just plans to read the list.

The girl understands she should read these books someday, or at least know what they're talking about.

These are the books? No one can believe it. They think of missing titles. They keep the list on hand, should they be tested. For most of August it sits on the fireplace table with the crumbs of cheese and crackers and marijuana, where Helen leans against an ugly new pillow without a loon. The list gets picked up and thrown down. It gathers a grease spot, an epoxy thumbprint, the almost-circle of a wine glass. Finally, someone mistakes it for trash.

Everyone blames JC, who can already recount the first 40 titles. He has a semi-photographic memory for words and a total photographic memory for numbers, he tells the girl. He hears a phone number once and knows it for life.

"How?" says the girl. She has someone to speak to now.

"I don't know," says JC. "It's annoying. I don't want them in there." He pauses to pick at something sticky from the table. "The numbers are colors, really."

The girl assumes this is because he smokes pot but it's a real thing, Ned says. It's called synesthesia.

"Your genius cousin," says Ned. He laughs. Because what would a genius be doing building a doomed airplane with a fat fuck like him?

But the girl remembers this, holds it close. Her cousin is a genius. Which means she could grow up to be a genius too.

The girl's father says they have to feed the puppy.

"He's not a puppy anymore," says the girl. But she gathers her sweatshirt and Speak and Spell and they leave.

●   ●   ●   ●

By the time the plane is done, the girl is a sophomore in college. JC is also in college, having decided to finish his engineering degree. Ned and Helen are footing the bill. Ned is so big he can no longer fit in the cockpit, but they fix this by moving the gearshift. Then Ned has gastric bypass surgery, just to be sure.

●   ●   ●   ●

Only Ned is at the camp on the day of the crash. JC has a new job in Portland where the pot is not so plentiful. Helen has gone to ride her horse, Hematite, in slow circles on a beautifully groomed pasture in Damariscotta, the next town over.

Ned wears jeans over his Speedos. The air is damp, the dock slick. The neighbor from New Jersey, leaning from his anchored Sunfish, waves with his baseball cap. Ned ignores him. The same neighbor has reported their wafting drug smells to the sheriff more than once.

Ned squeezes himself into the cockpit, taxis the plane to the far end of the lake. Through the warped plexiglass he sees the sturdy pines, the neat houses, his own house, the largest on the lake. The heat in that tight space makes him itch, makes him want to forget the whole thing and just dive in. But he accelerates. He rises like a bird might, skimming and skimming until there he is, lifted. The box he made carrying him out and above.

And down, as pine boughs crack. He clears his own dock by a few feet, smacking the water like a man inside a whale.

He pushes until his heart feels large, until he manages to snap open the cockpit door. He slices to the dock like an Olympian, *I'm a swimmer. A lifeguard. I taught the girl to dive.* The plane on its side in the mud is hooked by weeds but he can't think about that now. The neighbor jumps up and down from his boat but it's quiet in Ned's head, except for the chimes by the hammock, a sad little interval. Minor third, the girl has told him. Then the phone through the open screen begins to ring. Ned feels pressure in his ears and thinks, *organs.* There's a rushing sensation behind his forehead.

He stumbles to his van, reaches the Congressman's house before anyone else can find him. He bursts in, still wearing his waterlogged jeans, and heads to the fridge for a beer. The Congressman sits dry and poised in his armchair with a thick book, President Clinton's face on the cover. The girl, now a woman in complicated sandals, creeps up from her bedroom and stares.

"What happened?" she says.

"I need a toot," says Ned. He drinks. His voice sounds loud in the hole that is his brain. In this neat, brown house far from water. He remembers the epoxy stain he left in their bathtub. How the girl's mother made him clean it himself with steel wool.

"Your head," says the girl. "Something's bleeding."

He laughs. "I crashed the plane!"

"Why?" says the girl, and realizes this is the wrong question. *How,* she meant. How.

Her father doesn't move. The color in his cheeks is bright,

the expression new. His wrists are bandaged from recent carpel tunnel surgery.

Ned strides across the living room, his belly lunging, and grasps her father's fingers, lifting them to the streak on his forehead.

"*Don't you fucking touch me*," says the Congressman, little gunfire pellets of sound, and Ned laughs at the 'fucking' part, a bark so mean and otherworldly the girl doesn't know who to look at anymore.

"His wrists," says the girl, trying to explain. Her father tries to bend his thumbs in slow motion.

But Ned isn't looking at either of them anymore. He sits in the good chair, making it wet. He tips the bottle back and devises the first of many stories about the crash. That neighbor's sailboat, drifting from anchor and catching the airplane wing. A giant loon breaking its neck on the windshield. A comet singeing the pines in his path.

"Maybe you should lie down," says the daughter. "With some ice." But he only drinks in silence.

When he leaves, it looks like someone has peed in the chair. They stare at it for a while, father and daughter, until the van engine fades down their long dirt driveway.

They could blame the dog, forget this ever happened. But her father surprises her by saying, "I guess you won't ride in that plane." He laughs. His face is relaxed, his loose hands cradling the heavy book, his eyes bright but small behind the wrinkled lids.

"No one will ride in it," she says. *How did you get so old?*

She rises to grab a beer for herself. "Where's mom?" she asks.

Her father doesn't answer for a while. Then he looks at her, as though he's just remembered. "She went for a walk, I think."

•　　　•　　　•　　　•

Nine summers later, the woman decides to flee. She'll ask for the keys to Helen and Ned's New York City apartment because, like the girl in the Journey song, she needs to get out of her hometown or her head will explode. From her rent-free childhood bedroom, where she's slept for three months, she hears the blender whir, her father making shakes. Her boutonnière from prom is a brown, shrunken head on her mirrored bureau.

Her hometown is where she has no job but a new MFA, where her boyfriend of six years is no longer her boyfriend, where her father is getting chemotherapy and she can't allow herself to witness it, his steady disappearance. He'd skipped a treatment to come to her graduation. Now he wears the silk bathrobe she sent from Thailand and blends peanut butter and Hershey's syrup, the only food he's able to stomach. Ned offered pot but he still won't touch it.

Though he says nothing, she knows her father wants her to stay in the house with him. Instead she spends hours at Ocean Point in a foldable camping chair, where she reads beautifully sad books and fills a journal about the ex she cheated on. The sun smolders and the waves crash and crash. Too rough to swim.

She'll ask Ned for the apartment keys, not Helen. Ned can be swayed because of the swimming lessons and the ax, because of the monogrammed stationery he gave her and the careful note: *Carpe diem.* She'd never been a child to him but a small person who didn't know enough yet.

She'll be beholden, like JC, who accepted the gifts of college tuition and Lasik eye surgery. But Manhattan. It seems like a worthwhile trade.

●　　　●　　　●　　　●

At the camp there's a breeze, dainty marks on the water. The sad cluck of the minor, rusted chimes. The hammock looks wet. Helen is far away on the dock in an orange one-piece, an arm flung over her face, her body so still she must be sleeping.

"How old are you now?" Ned says. Two roach clips shine on the picnic table like earrings. He doesn't offer a hit.

"Twenty-eight," she tells him.

"Shit," he says. He's still large, despite the surgery, though no one understands how this is possible. His beard is not yet grey. He takes out the pocket watch, finds the buried key ring in his flannel pocket, places it on the table and not in her hand. She takes it quickly, before he changes his mind.

"You have a month," he says. It's mid-August. Helen is taking a sabbatical, so they don't have to rush back for her classes this year. Ned will speak to his patients by phone until they return.

He tells his theory about New York City, that it's impossible to have everything at the same time there—the job, the apartment, the relationship. Something has to give.

His other theory is that people from small towns are what keep Manhattan in business. The pounding of her pillow at night has not been in vain. She is part of an ongoing tradition.

"How's your father?" he says as she gets up.

"I don't really know." She watches as Helen stirs on the dock but doesn't rise. She digs the teeth of one key into her thumb.

"Chemo." He whistles down the scale.

"Yes." She's losing this conversational round but it's all she has to offer.

•   •   •   •

A friend from grad school picks her up at Penn Station and gapes at the odd plushness inside the apartment. Mirrored walls, red shag carpet, silver ceilings. The wall of tropical plants she's supposed to water. A large H and N above the bed, which JC cut from plywood and spray-painted purple.

"Soul Train," says the friend.

"Solid Gold," says the girl. "Solid Gold dancers."

The friend leaves and there's a long stretch of otherworldly time—an hour, perhaps—during which the girl understands, *I have no idea how to do this*. She's supposed to make it here. This is her mother's town. She begins to panic in earnest then, a pulse she sees as green inside, charging through her limbs and making it hard to control her heart. She has to move, moving is good. Stillness is how people get sick.

She prepares, finds her laminated street map, small enough to be discreet. She carries the silver whistle on a string from her father, leaves behind the mace spray. She adopts the expression of a non-tourist—bored, competent—and steps outside into the South Street Seaport. Cobbled streets and a looming old ship called *The Peking*, docked for the visitors eating ice cream. A Disneyfied version of Maine. The tourists wear the items she refused to pack: practical walking shoes, windbreakers in bright colors. They tip the Statue of Liberty mime and the busker strumming "American Pie" and aren't afraid to gawk. She will not gawk, even though there are water taxis and famous buildings and a beer stand.

She buys her first Manhattan beer in a big plastic cup, tips the pimply man a dollar and drinks quickly. She eats a slice of pizza on a bench and the broccoli feels like the fingertip of a dish glove. It's the most important piece of pizza she's eaten.

Back in the apartment, buzzed, she can drop the bored face. She lands on the red couch, sinking in, and devises a timeline. She wants to show how resourceful she is. Two weeks seems like a reasonable amount of time to land a job and an apartment. She has an MFA. She knows 300 pop songs by heart. Surely there's a place for her somewhere on this island.

In the morning she spends several hours in the Strand Bookstore Annex reading the diaries of Anaïs Nin. She forgets to buy milk. As evening comes, she wanders down to the cobbled streets again, past the Gap and J. Crew to watch the black, shining water. This time she understands she's seeing the lights of New Jersey on the other side. Then she's at the beer stand again, paying the boy, who doesn't seem to recognize her. She finds the same backless wooden bench facing the hulk of buildings and from there she sees the stacks of lit-up rooms. Offices. In college, when she'd tried to be a secretary for her parents, it had taken a long time to file things correctly. They didn't suggest it the following year. But maybe she's faster now. Maybe she'll end up in an office wearing her pale pink jacket and matching skirt. Low heels. She'll find a temp agency to-morrow and inquire.

Instead she calls ex-boyfriends from college. Two live in the city now—one in the East Village, one in Midtown. She'll bring them to the cheap Thai place around the corner, then the beer stand. They'll sit close on the bench and look at tall build-ings and drink and reminisce and the end of summer coolness will make them sit closer and she won't have to sleep in the strange porn set apartment alone.

"You've done this before," the second one says on the beer bench.

"With my girlfriend from grad school," she lies.

Two weeks turn into three. She calls the boyfriends until one tells her to stop calling. He's not looking for a relationship right now. Who said she's looking for a relationship? Who says he gets to decide how things turn out? She calls to tell him this and he hangs up and she cries and cries and takes out her laptop for the first time since arriving and writes and writes until she realizes she needs water, she needs to eat. It's too late for the beer stand, the pizza stand, so she wolfs two large bowls of Cheerios and opens an expensive-looking bottle from Helen and Ned's towering silver wine rack. She backs up the file on floppy disc, pleased to have turned the angst into fiction. She's on a roll here. She has come to New York City to be an artist, of course she has. She has an MFA.

Her sleep is heavy and uncomplicated. The hard mattress faces the window and through the slats of morning she hears a sound that may be part of her sleeping brain. It's a meteor falling, the cartoon whistle of it, followed by a Bugs Bunny crash. She sleeps again. Then there are seagulls, hundreds of them squawking, the sound of summer at Ocean Point when too many people are eating sandwiches—how the birds descend, just like in the movie, and the eaters have to flap them away with their hands.

Then she's awake and hears sirens, not birds.

In the living room she sees a blotch of cartoon sky—blue with glitter, shiny particles dancing like Glinda. There is commotion in the courtyard, where a man says, "How could a plane just miss?" The man sounds like Ned, though of course he can't be. Ned is in his lake house in Maine, his own plane already broken.

She can't see anything beyond the blue patch and the courtyard. She can't figure out how to turn on the TV, three remotes, so she plugs in the dusty radio. Jazzed morning DJs speak as though they're being paid by the word.

She tries to call her parents and Ned but she can't get through.

She calls the friend from grad school who says, "Close the windows, turn off the AC. Not to sound weird, but does it seem as though it might fall on you?"

"What?"

"The building."

She's not yet scared because she doesn't understand what it means—no one does. She packs a bag, things she might need. Birth control pills, toothbrush, socks. Laptop? She can't decide.

Amphibians

She keeps bumping into things, whacking body parts into hard edges. The glass table, the mirrored column. Later she'll discover a bowl-sized bruise on her thigh.

The DJs can't believe it when another meteor lands. This isn't an accident. They start using the word, *attack*.

The blue patch is gone. Gray now, smoky.

Eventually—how much time passes?—a rumble like the earth opening, like Superman and the jagged split of earthquake with things falling down into the pit that is the center of below. (What is that feeling? Relief? Something definitive is happening—she has to make a choice.) She bolts, then goes back to get the keys. Did she lock the door? She doesn't know. As she runs the length of hallway and sees someone ahead of her, leaping for the stairs, a leg attached to what must be another human. She needs to see people—as many of them as she can stand. They stream through the courtyard now, people with expensive, dusty shoes. She wears a black sweatshirt that is hers, not Helen's, and covers her mouth with the sleeve. She asks a police officer what do to, stay or go? He doesn't answer. He's busy talking to a small crowd around him. She doesn't want to go. But she follows the people filing through with briefcases. Calm, open faces, looking at each other, not bored, because this is not an ordinary day.

The only person shouting is an old lady in an apron. "Walk, don't run!" She has set up a little station with folding chairs, water pitchers, plastic cups. She grabs the girl's arm. "Help me tell them," she says. The girl obeys, though no one is running.

"Walk, don't run." She feels foolish. She's not loud enough and it's not what she would choose to tell them right now. The smoke is thicker and she looks at the old woman to try to explain but she's not paying attention.

The girl runs away again, back against the tide of people to

Ned and Helen's lobby, and she has to sit on the floor inside to breathe. There are other dazed people in there, men. No one asks if she's okay.

"They never should have let those people in," someone says. She doesn't say anything. She has to get away from the people saying *those people*.

She climbs the stairs and sees no one in the hall.

Inside seems safer, although there is the burning smell from outside. The burning of matter that is not supposed to be. She can't think about this yet. She calls her mother, gets through, can't really hear what her mother is saying. "I'm bored," she says into the phone. "I have to wait in here." Why does she say this?

Then her cell battery is dead. The subways are down, the landlines out, the bridges and tunnels closed to vehicles. She will likely lose electricity, says Peter Jennings, whom she believes to be her friend. She fills pots with water. She listens to Peter Jennings until the radio batteries die too.

She could walk to New Jersey, to her grad school friend, but she doesn't really know the way, even with her laminated map. And even in these circumstances, a part of her would rather be alone, rather not have to make conversation that isn't real.

The sweatshirt sleeve where she made an *O* of her mouth is a different color, darker than the rest of the sweatshirt now. The rest of the sleeve looks like it's been used to mop a high shelf. There was a book she read. *Tiger's Eye?* Someone saves a paper bag with the father's bloody clothes—what he wore the night he was killed. The teenage daughter finds the bag, crusted, and it's the worst thing. Evidence of a body that once was.

Even if she washes the sweatshirt she'll think of what's been removed each time she wears it. Particles. She takes it off, pushes it into the garbage under the sink on top of paper towels and soggy Cheerios she couldn't swallow. She stands in the dark space in just her bra until she understands that she is cold.

•　　•　　•　　•

In the morning she walks until she finds a working pay phone. Fifteen blocks. She walks to the ex-boyfriend's place, the one who still takes her calls. He constructs a tuna sandwich from stale bread and salad dressing and they quickly run out of things to say. She can't stay there and she doesn't have to. Her father has already found an empty apartment his client owns in Tudor City, right next to the UN.

Her father's voice on the phone is trying to be blank like Helen's. He tells her, if she must stay in New York City, to consider an outer borough, some place not dependent on bridges and tunnels to get her home. To Maine, he means. His voice is not convincing. He's breaking with every word.

She buys cheap clothes from Conway's, two outfits she'll wear again and again. She spends her days with newspapers in Central Park reading every page, even the ads, trying to make her brain understand the words. There are Missing Persons posters tacked to walls. There are tanks surrounding the UN. There's no need for more blood donations. She hates needles; she's a fainter. But she was willing to give it a try.

When she finds her own apartment, a studio in Hell's Kitchen, the broker decides to waive the finder's fee because of where she's from, which is "Downtown."

I'm from Maine, she doesn't say.

Some people are using the term already, Ground Zero, but she resists. It sounds like a Hollywood fiction.

She sits in a metal folding chair the previous tenant left behind, labeled *PS183* in black Sharpie on the back, which she knows is shorthand for the school down the block. Pre-teens stream past at 3:00 pm on weekdays and ring her buzzer over and over again. It's cheerful at first. She peers from behind the purple tie-dyed sheet that is her curtain and sees their over-sized backpacks, their complicated hairstyles, the slouch of the boys, the girls looking wiser. Did one of them take the chair out of school on a dare, carry it down the street to lean against her stoop?

Are they nervous about their days now? Do they have curfews?

She wonders if she will know people soon.

The landlord calls to tell her to take down the god-awful sheet, this isn't a college dorm.

•   •   •   •

Ned and Helen decide to extend their time in Maine. They ask her to check on the apartment, once she's allowed to go back below 14th street.

She finds, in the Fulton Street subway stop, the smell of burning still. It's like the smell of Das Boot, but less chemical—more like dirt, of the earth, which makes no sense until she realizes, again, that so many kinds of matter turned to ash that day, not just office supplies and furniture.

The smell makes the commuters quiet. It smells like it will never go away.

Above ground, some stores are open again. She wants not to look but she looks at the place in the skyline where there's nothing now.

In the apartment there's black dust everywhere because she left a window open. Just a crack. She vacuums, washes sheets, washes brown towels. The neighbor has been watering the plants but she waters them all again. She empties the sour milk, sorts the recycling, pulls the threads of her hair that have woven themselves into the red couch. *Traces,* she thinks. Should she ever try to disappear, they'd see where she'd been.

Amphibians

When she locks the door behind, she tries to summon the new, stupid anxiety of her first day there, six weeks ago.

She wonders if the beer stand is open. Of course not. She splurges on a cab, which takes a while to hail.

•   •   •   •

Ned drives the van from Maine with a second-hand armchair the color of a rotting pumpkin. He double parks outside her stoop and says, "You're doing it, kid. You got the apartment." He didn't think she'd actually stay. How much is she paying in rent?

And then he drives, without her, to Katz's for a pastrami sandwich.

•   •   •   •

For Thanksgiving in Maine, everyone crams into the van to pick her up at the Greyhound terminal—her father, mother, JC, Helen, Ned, plus the new dog, bought to replace her. Her father blinks fast. He is shrinking. Her mother scans her face for signs of breakage. In the van there are strange pauses the girl is causing. No one mentions that day.

At the table, after the meal, Ned asks how much she makes at her temp job, how much she pays in rent. You can't have everything at the same time: the job, the apartment, the relationship. Something has to give.

She doesn't want to tell him how much but she isn't quick enough to lie. Does this make her a prude? She owes them. She left the window open.

Ned's lids are heavy. "We have no idea who you are," he says, sweeping his arm across the table to include the turkey bones, the crusted gravy boat, his wife, who tries to look away from both of them. Her parents are stacking dishes in the kitchen and can't save her. JC has already gone back to Portland for the night.

Amphibians

The girl leans in, her heart fast. "So ask me," she says, a crack allowing the steam to vent. The voice doesn't belong to her.

Ned laughs, the same huge bellow, and soon he passes out on the couch with Helen, their legs interlocked like spiders.

●　　　●　　　●　　　●

Her mother suggests it a few times and so, back in Manhattan, the girl agrees to see a shrink. He looks at his watch and seems not to hear when the girl reveals she walked eighty-three blocks to the appointment in order to avoid the subway.

But eventually he looks up from his pad. "Do you think that's unusual?"

"The bomb threat in London. On the Tube," she tries to explain. Her father sent her an email about this.

"No one else I've seen today has mentioned it," he says.

Which she interprets as, *Stop whining. We were all here that day.*

She takes the subway back, but it's not easy. There are smells she can't identify and nervous men with big backpacks who could be hiding things. She turns up her iPod and in blares Prince, something innocuous about rough sex and tangerines.

●　　　●　　　●　　　●

Her father receives a clean bill of health. To celebrate, he drinks sparkling cider with her mother. They take a photo and send it via email. The girl sends a card with sunflowers and does the math. He's 80 years old now.

●　　　●　　　●　　　●

Helen and Ned return to their apartment, which they hire someone to clean professionally, and invite the girl out to dinner on weekends. It's important to support the businesses downtown, they say. The beer piles up. Full, untouched pint glasses next to her plate. Ned orders bacon, fries, extra mushrooms, all the things she doesn't want to consume but consumes because they're right in front of her.

Ned insults the waiter and the girl apologizes, sneaking back in to tip him well. Ned uses the n-word, the c-word, blurting out to be seen in those loud, dark places.

"You're too polite," he complains. He sits like a fat man, legs splayed to make room for his girth, though he'll never be quite as fat as he once was.

She tries to change the subject. She talks about books, museums, her new ESL students.

He speaks to Helen as though the girl isn't there. "She's an intellectual now. We just pretend to be."

"Speak for yourself," says Helen. She tries to look at the girl but her head wobbles. She's read all the books on the list by now, she means.

He says it again, "Helen and I—we have no idea who you are," and it's the pairing that gets to her, *Helen and I*, when there's so little they seem to agree on. She'd been pondered and discussed. The conclusion was so obvious they didn't need to take sides.

She gets up and reaches for her purse, one practiced motion. She's a New Yorker now. In Maine you can dawdle, leave it hanging on the edge of your chair as you fiddle with your coat, your scarf. But here it's best never to lose contact. She leaves her coat. Ned's arms are folded. His neck is perfectly still.

"You're going," he says. He doesn't seem surprised.

She loses her nerve then.

"I'm going to the bathroom," she says. She does this. She tries to breathe in there. How many times has she hidden in stalls for things to make sense, until it's safe for her to return without screaming? They'd like her more if she came out screaming,

someone they resemble. Her mother can do this, insert herself
into hard conversations with the right balance of playfulness
and indignation, smiling as she delivers the insult, throwing
them off balance. They love her for it. They don't recognize the
sting until later. Or they don't remember.

She joins them at the table again. They drink. Then it surg-
es inside her again, the need to flee. She stands. She hasn't
stopped holding her purse.

"I'm leaving," she says. "I can't do it anymore—the way
you—I actually can't stand you anymore."

Helen looks up, her mouth a circle.

Ned laughs. There's glee in the sound. They have broken her
at last.

On the quiet street, a shine on the slick black sidewalk. The
financiers have gone home. A cab comes quickly and in the
back seat she waits for her phone to ring, for Helen to ask her
to come back, please, it's all been a misunderstanding. They
love her like a daughter, the daughter they never had.

She checks—yes, her phone is on.

She dials her mother instead, begins to cry, pauses to yell at
the cabbie to take East Broadway instead.

"Sleep on it," says her mother. "See how you feel in the
morning." She's a diplomat, a good lawyer. She doesn't put the
girl's father on the phone.

In the morning, the girl writes a passive aggressive letter
and sends it registered receipt. *This is what it means to be rich.
Clothes with stains and a fat gold ring. A lack of concern about
wreckage. So what if the float has a hole? Ruin is part of it, part of
the fun. Ruin is what you can afford.*

She's surprised when they don't reply.

She assumes she'll see them near the Seaport or at Katz's.
She thinks, when her first book comes out, they'll send a

monogrammed note.

When she sees them by chance in her hometown bar, back in Maine to visit her mother, her father gone now for two years, she gathers the chutzpah to tap Helen on the shoulder.

Helen turns to look, her eyes clear and sorry. "I was sad to hear about your father," she says. She's drinking something that looks like seltzer and lime. She wears glasses with funky purple frames and the same large, gold ring. Her hair is its natural shade, white. Her lush leather purse hangs on the back of her chair for anyone to steal.

"Can I join you?" says the girl. It's Christmas, the small lights in the bar white and warm. There are so many words and the girl is ready now. She can speak to them.

"No," says Ned, his back to her.

The girl tries to stay perfectly still. She thinks to take the purse and run. Instead, she sits in her car and cries until her breath fogs up the windows, until she's too snotty to breathe well, too cold to be still. She's had too much to drink. She drives slowly and isn't pulled over.

•　　•　　•　　•

At 37, the girl quits her no-where job, gives up the apartment and leaves Manhattan for a small New England town with mountains instead of sea. She finds yoga and meets a man who sees her clearly, asks her questions. She goes out to hear the man play guitar with his band, and because of the sexiness of being outside in late summer, because of the white wine buzz and the symmetrical stone and wire fire pit with fake coals and real heat, because of people at tables talking loudly and ignoring the music, she thinks of Helen, drunk on the lake in late summer. She can feel what Helen must have felt, the softness of the air and the necessary distance from the complications on the dock. How the child—not her own—must have been a welcome distraction at times.

She wonders if, at the end of August, there's still skinny-dip-
ping, the sky purple, the top leaves almost red, the mosquitoes
interested. They had to take off their suits first, then jump.
Even her father did it. There were jokes about man parts shriv-
eling as the couples found each other, slick and familiar.

She wasn't cold. They were somewhere in the dark, within
reach. (Voices, splashing.) How easy the water felt against her
open skin. How she stayed away from them, treading.

Dishdash

Mo perches on a barstool in Dubai and listens to the Emirati man sitting beside her. He's speaking about a song he likes, an Arabic song. Mo isn't sure why. She's jet-lagged and spacey and a little drunk, already. She's had an entire glass of white wine in the space of twenty minutes and the edges of things are pleasantly blurred.

Mo is waiting for her brother Mickey, the Bar Manager, to finish his shift. He took an X-Acto knife "out back" and she imagines that he's now slicing cardboard boxes and taking stock. Until he'd appeared at the Dubai International Airport that afternoon, Mo hadn't seen her brother in two years.

The Emirati man next to Mo wears a long white robe and a white headscarf folded in complicated ways. A snaked, black coil balances on the narrow crown of his head. "It is the most beautiful song," the Emirati man is saying. "Really, you *must* believe me." He cracks a pistachio nut from a tiny brass bowl and chews. "I will bring the song for you tomorrow." He signals to the Filipino barman with a pointed finger and another round is poured.

Mo has to pee. She wishes her brother would hurry up and be done. "I won't be here tomorrow," she says to the man. She came for sun and distraction, not for men in robes. She came for Mickey.

"Anyway, the song means your name, in Arabic," the Emirati continues. *"Lura."* He clicks the 'L' into place and makes a little 'o' of his mouth, room enough for a nut. *"Lu*-ra," he says again.

"My name?" Mo asks.

He'll try to find a recording in the Citi Center shopping mall, he says, perhaps in the Music Master shop. The song is by a famous Saudi Arabian singer, he says. *"Very* famous."

There's something Mo should tell the man: *My name isn't Laura. It's* Maura, *actually. Maureen,* but she doesn't correct him. She wants to sustain the confusion. She likes the thought of having her own song.

Encouraged by Mo's silence, the man begins to write the first verse of the song on a napkin, in Arabic. To Mo it looks like squiggles either way, from right to left or left to right. The song is long and very slow, says the man. About half an hour.

"Half an hour?" Mo asks. "Wow." She sips her white wine, her ankles crossed. She steals a glance at his pen—it's shiny, maybe even real gold. He presses the point to the napkin and the ink bleeds.

The man peers over the top of his eyeglasses to translate what he's written but he can't seem to make it out. He's too tipsy now, he says, laughing, enjoying this strange word, tipsy, then refills his glass from the bottle of Beck's. "I will write it better tomorrow."

"Time to cut you off," says Mickey, appearing. Speaking to Mo. A joke.

"We should go home," Mo says. She tries to remember the name of the Emirati man, to thank him for the drink, but she can't.

•   •   •   •

After work, Mo and Mickey sit close together on the pullout

sofa in Mickey's apartment. They drink warm Heineken from the bottles he stole from work as the TV screen shows a page from the Quran.

"Prayer time," Mickey explains, and a singer wails in the background. He presses a button on the remote and the wailing stops. "You were bored tonight," he says.

Mo blinks back with effort, forcing her eyes to focus. She's too tired to disagree. She thinks of the Emirati, clearly a regular. "You'll be a hit with the regulars," Mickey had promised.

Mo pulls at a thread on her blouse. It doesn't snap off, just gets longer and longer but she can't stop pulling.

Mickey considers the label on his bottle and picks at a corner with a trimmed nail. He sips again.

The details can wait, Mo thinks. They've got all week and she'll get the whole story out of him eventually: why he came, exactly, why he decided to stay, when he's coming back. She doesn't have to make sense of these things all at once. She isn't sure she's able.

"There weren't any women in the bar," Mo remembers.

"There are sometimes," says Mickey, careful not to say *women* himself.

When she'd called to give him her flight details, she'd mentioned "the women down the hall" and she felt him bristle. *Oh, you're among* women *now, are you? Not girls?* She liked the thought of him bristling. Usually it was the other way around.

She studies his profile as he tips back the bottle—the rigid jaw, the black hair. He's stocky, his chest compact, his arms solid. She sees him at age six, clutching a red plastic wrench on Christmas morning and yelling, "I'll unscrew your belly-button!" She'd slept with her hands tight on her belly for a week.

Mickey says she looks different, older. Has she done something new?

Dishdash

"Not really."

She's all angles, he says, like she's lost weight. Has she?

"Just exam stress," she says. "You remember."

He frowns a little. College wasn't a high point for him.

It bothers him, she knows, how fundamentally different their bodies are—her height, her boniness. He thinks it's an illusion, thinks that underneath she's tough, sturdy, and that it's his duty to shake the sturdiness out of her. She lets him think this. She doesn't want to fight right now, to defend her anatomy.

Instead she describes the flight attendants, how they wore little caps with veils.

"I know," says Mickey.

Some of the passengers went to the bathroom wearing jeans and came out wearing their national dress, she continues, the men in white *dishdashes* and the women in black *abayas*. (This Mo had read in her *Lonely Planet*. The United Arab Emirates guide was the thinnest of all *Lonely Planets* on the bookstore shelf.) In person, on the plane, the men looked priestly. It was hard not to stare, hard not to think of what they might look like underneath their robes. The women showed only their eyes and Mo felt a little whorish in her tee shirt.

"Whorish," Mickey repeats.

She nods.

During the descent the sand looked like it was creeping in, taking over roads. (This Mo keeps to herself.) She'd thought, *They must have to work very hard to sweep it all back.* She'd remembered a faded yellow cover and her mother reading aloud.

> If seven maids with seven mops
> Should try for half a year,
> Do you suppose, the Walrus said,
> That they could get it clear?

49

Amphibians

Mickey had hated the *Alice* books. He liked *Star Wars*. For Halloween he'd been Chewbacca three years in a row.

Mickey first came to Dubai straight after sophomore year, just for a laugh, he'd told Mo. His roommate at U. Maine knew someone who knew someone who'd made it big in the oil game and was now part owner of The Club. "The job's yours if you want it," the roommate said. "They'll love your accent over there."

"The oil game?" Mickey's father had asked.

It was supposed to be for the summer, but Mickey stayed through the fall and the spring. He deferred for one year and then another, but he didn't mention school on the phone to Mo. He said, "Dubai is it. Good money, no taxes, warm weather." He'd apply for permanent residency if The Club agreed to sponsor him.

And now Mo was the one in school, wanting a break. "If you come, I'll take you out," he'd promised. "The clubs are *fab*."

Fab, Mo thinks to herself now. *What a funny little word.* She leans her head back on the sofa and Mickey eases the bottle from her slack hand.

•　　　•　　　•　　　•

Mo had met someone named Kyle early in the semester, and she wanted to describe him to Mickey in more detail. Kyle had bushy brown curls and a wicked grin, amazing teeth. He had this jittery, energetic way about him, like a force jerking through his blood. He played the saxophone.

Kyle invited Mo to a Gamelan concert the weekend before Valentine's Day. Mo had never heard of the Gamelan, and it turned out to be an Indonesian instrument, or many instruments acting as one, all percussive—bells and gongs and cymbals—all metallic and cheerful-sounding. The musicians either stood or sat cross-legged on the floor, mallets poised. There were dozens of them.

Dishdash

"It's cyclical," Kyle explained. "Each player is assigned a place in the sequence." One hit a gong every fourth beat, one every eighth, and so on.

Mo liked the idea of it, the interlocking rhythms. She watched the one with the biggest gong, large as a tabletop, shiny as tin foil. He had to wait sixty-four beats—she counted—and when he did it the noise he made was a shimmering ripple.

"*Yeah*," Kyle said. He closed his eyes and she watched them flicker underneath the lids. His lashes were long and pretty and Mo had an urge to lick them.

He had needles in his dorm room, stacked in neat plastic packages on the bookshelf. Mo tried not to look at them but he told her anyway: diabetes. She thought this might explain the jerkiness. *You might die young,* she thought. Was that a relief? Did it make him braver with the small stuff, like sex, like music? She hated needles. She would have to learn to live with them, she thought. She'd have to watch him stick himself daily.

But she didn't have to. He invited her back to his room only once more. He'd put up a giant poster of John Coltrane, his sax collar dangling, his eyes huge and sad against a dark blue background.

"Is he your idol?" she asked, teasing.

He shrugged.

Could they just be friends? He didn't say this in the room, but on the phone the next day, his voice a little sour, a little tired. In need of sugar.

A week later she called Mickey in Dubai. She'd been to a party, she'd had too much beer—she wanted to hear a dumb joke about musicians, if he had any.

Instead he said, "You're too intense, Mo. It scares guys off. You need to chill out a little." That's when he said she should come to Dubai. He described a bar he'd take her to, called TGIT, Thank God It's Thursday.

"Friday," she corrected.

"No, Thursday. Friday's the Holy Day, the big day off. The point is, it's a bar."

"I'll come," she said, quickly. "How much are flights?"

Mo's roommate said, "You're lucky. There's no way I could spend spring break with my brother. We'd kill each other."

"We're pretty close," Mo explained. She wasn't sure if this was still true.

Mickey had called when he was drunk once, when he was a freshman and Mo was still living at home. He was sobbing. He'd failed his exams. "Listen to me," he said, "crying like a girl."

She'd felt relieved. It had been difficult to keep the smugness out of her voice, not because he'd failed, but because he was crying.

•   •   •   •

Mo wakes up late on Mickey's sofa bed, her neck stiff, her head sore. She makes coffee and snoops through drawers, finding little of interest. It's a boy's apartment, sparse, smelling of feet. There are nine back issues of *For Him Magazine,* stacked carefully under his bed.

Mickey is on a day shift today, so she won't have to sit in the bar tonight, waiting for him. "Go to the pool," he suggested, and left the keys.

The pool is on the roof of a hotel down the street and all the tenants in Mickey's building are allowed to use it. "They won't ask," he said, but he left his pass anyway.

Outside the heat is startling. Mo's sunglasses fog up and her air-conditioned bones heat up fast. Within one block she's baking, straight through. The sand gets in her new leather sandals. The sand is everywhere, it seems, blowing onto sidewalks and sweeping over the vacant lots between apartment blocks. It's not gritty like sand at home, but fine and feather-white, like dust.

She slows her pace, like everyone else, to a lazy shuffle, a trudge, and it feels wrong, unsafe. She's used to walking briskly, eyes ahead—her city walk. "The trick is not to *fight* the heat," said Mickey, "just accept it." The local men, all in white, seem to glide through it. *Biblical-looking*, Mo thinks, *with black coils for crowns.*

There are no other women on the street, and so the men in white notice her. A black Jeep Cherokee slows and the driver's mouth under the headscarf says something she doesn't understand. She stares back from behind her sunglasses and he grins even harder. She turns her head and he drives away.

She remembers the Emirati in the bar, how polite he seemed. Educated at Cambridge, he'd told her. He would've been robeless in England. He would've worn jeans for the first time, and sweaters.

She passes a Holiday Inn and the Al Medina 24-Hour Store, the neon lights flashing even at noon. A crane roars and Indian workers shout from ladders and in concrete pits. They're not speaking to her (in Hindi? In Urdu?) but to each other. She can smell the sweat as she passes. "In the summer they hire twice as many," Mickey told her, so when one faints from the heat another can take his place. From a taxi the day before she saw them shoved into an open-back truck, slouching, dozing, saying nothing.

"It can't be legal," Mo had said to her brother.

"It's Dubai," Mickey had said.

The receptionist in the pool hotel checks her pass and waves her toward the elevator. In the lobby cafe there are two canaries in a cage, one yellow, one blue. Mo watches them twitter and peep, comforted, until the elevator dings.

She has the pool to herself, a great relief. She peels away her tee shirt and shorts and adjusts her bikini top. The sign says, "Appropriate Swim-Wear Required," and she wonders if her bikini is appropriate. "I've seen girls in tee shirts and sweat-pants in the sea," Mickey said.

The water is icy-cold, clean. The chlorine smell is strong. From the shallow end she can see the street she's just passed, sees that it's crowded with pastel buildings further along, and high-rises with shiny reflective glass, and that these are interspersed with sandy vacant patches, spaces not yet cov-ered with tar. The sand seems harmless from this height, not pretty exactly, but natural. Proof of a Bedouin past.

She doesn't stay long. Within minutes her skin feels tight and burned and she can't concentrate on her book. It's creepy up there alone, looking down at the cranes. On her way back some of the workmen are asleep on the sidewalk on strips of cardboard, arms slung over their eyes, feet splayed. Dead-look-ing. There are little silver lunch-box tins at their sides.

In the apartment Mo rubs the white sand from her shoes and it leaves brown streaks on the towel, like ordinary dirt. She drinks an entire can of Pepsi and reads, in *Lonely Planet*, that Dubai is "the Miami of the Middle East." She falls asleep on the couch, waiting for Mickey to come back home.

•   •   •   •

When Mo was eleven, they went on family trip to Florida, to see Nana. It was Easter break and the beach was packed. There was a boardwalk along the street and Mo wanted to walk a portion of it, the part within view. Dad said fine, have fun. He smiled more in Florida. He said yes to things.

It was late afternoon and the beach was slowly clearing out. There were occasional speed walkers and joggers along the boardwalk, and a few older women strolling with visors, animated and loud. Mo didn't have sneakers with her, just flip-flops, but she walked briskly, with purpose, as the exercisers did. Her skin tingled with sunburn. It was nice to be alone.

She didn't immediately see the man on the bench. He was petting something in his lap, a puppy or a kitten, cooing at it, grunting a little. She looked, and saw instead his pants at his ankles, gray pubic hair, his penis gripped in his hand.

She felt something like panic then, a controlled panic, a rush of fear and adrenaline and a voice in her head saying, *Run*. She ran, back to the cluster of towels and coolers and people she knew.

How strange, she thought much later. *The instinct to flee. The complete lack of indecision.*

She told Mickey about it that night in Nana's guest room. There were two cots set up in a space meant for one. She could just make out the outline of his body opposite her, under a sleeping bag. The ceiling fan whirred above them in the dark.

"I would have kicked his ass," Mickey whispered, "if I'd been there. *Sicko*."

He was quiet for a long time. Mo thought he was asleep but then he giggled.

"What?" she asked.

"Nothing."

"*What?*" She'd kill him for laughing at her.

"I can't believe you thought it was a puppy."

She laughed too, a burst of relieved giggles. Then she eased into sleep, slowly, listening to him breathe beside her.

•　　　•　　　•　　　•

Mickey has another late shift and Mo resumes her perch at the bar.

"I have looked it up in English for you," says the Emirati man.

Amphibians

What? Mo thinks.

"You must recall. This Persian song, called 'Lo-ra.'"

She nods, remembering. She wants to see the gold pen again.

"In English this means *yogurt*."

Mo scrunches her brow in an expression of interest.

"Or not yogurt, exactly. Something between yogurt and milk."

"Cream?" says Mo. The wine arrives and she grabs the glass like a child.

"Not cream. Something thicker than milk, but not cream." He lifts the edge of his headscarf away from his face, a practiced gesture, and it stays there, balanced on the black coil. "Anyway, I will find the audio for you."

When he gives her the CD, the next night, the singer on the cover looks like he can't possibly be famous—he's wearing the same thing as every other Emirati she's met so far, except the singer's head scarf is red and white checked, instead of plain white.

"Abdu," says the man. "He is very famous."

"Mohammed Abdul," she repeats.

"Not Abdul. Ab-*doo*."

The CD is from the Citi Center Mall, he says. "Have you been there? You must go. Every shop you can imagine. Tell your brother to take you there."

Mo imagines this man taking the escalator, in the mall. He would have to lift his robe a little, like a woman lifting a long skirt over a puddle.

She looks around for Mickey, but he isn't in the bar—he's unpacking bottles again or sneaking a cigarette. Through the glass doors she sees the front patio with the empty wicker tables and chairs, abandoned in the heat, and the fountain which she knows is stuffed with fat, orange fish, so many fish they slide against one another, a slick mass of bodies trying to find air and space of their own.

"Disgusting," Mo announced, during daylight, during Mickey's grand tour the first afternoon.

"They fuck a lot. They replicate."

"They don't do that. They have eggs."

"The eggs need to be fertilized. What do you think, they just appear, like pimples?"

"Nice," said Mo. "Nice imagery."

He was feeding the fish at the time, thick flakes of something that looked like cereal.

Maybe he fell in, she thinks now at the bar. Maybe the fish are eating him alive.

Help me, she thinks. *Wonder Twin power, activate.* But he doesn't appear.

The regular introduces Mo to his friends in the bar. They're called Hamaid, Hamad, Abdullah and Fahim.

"Hello," says Mo. She remembers to show her teeth when she smiles.

The friends speak to her in English and to him in Arabic, but she knows they're talking about her by the way their eyes flick across her body, the way they turn away from her when they laugh. "Little sister!" they say and they think this is funny because she's taller than Mickey.

They ask questions and she answers. She's on vacation, she says, from college. In Boston. She grew up in Maine. *Maine.* Near Canada. That's right, Stephen King.

Someone mentions the Salem Witch Trials and then someone else says that maybe she's a witch and then someone else says, no, she can't be a witch because she's much too beautiful, and besides, she has blonde hair. She doesn't tell them it's dyed.

The friends mingle and disperse. Another glass of Chardonnay appears.

"You know, I am here every night," the Arab man tells her. "Every night but Friday."

Amphibians

His eyes, Mo decides, are kind-looking.

He has a wife, he says, and Mo wonders if the wife is at home now, waiting. She imagines the wife in the servants' quarters, knocking on the door of the pool boy or the driver, her black *abaya* falling to the floor like an empty cape.

He's just being friendly, Mo tells herself. *Bar talk.* She puts the CD in her purse and sips her wine. Mickey, at some point, will be able to fill in the gaps, to explain.

After work, Mickey takes her to a place called Stayin' Alive, which turns out to be a seventies-themed club, with a band. The guitarist wears a pink shirt with a John Travolta collar and the lead singer wears a tight silver jumpsuit. The door-man doesn't bother checking their IDs because their skin is white—this is Mickey's explanation. Inside she sees no Indians or Pakistanis or Filipinos. It's one of the most popular clubs in Dubai, Mickey says.

It's Ladies' Night, and so the dance floor is packed with slim, tan British and Australian girls in miniskirts and spaghet-ti-strap tank tops. All drinks are half-price for ladies, all night.

"It's not fair," Mickey shouts above the music. "They should have a Men's Night too!"

He buys two bottles of beer and leaves the change. Someone on the dance floor has noticed him already.

"Go on, dance if you want," Mo shouts.

"You sure?" he says, but he's already set his bottle down on the bar. "I know her," he explains. "She's a stewardess for Emirates Air."

"Flight attendant," Mo says, but he's gone. Mo's long-sleeved shirt is wrong. She isn't showing enough skin. But she drinks quickly, and by the time Mickey comes back, she feels better.

"Let's do shots!" he says. His shirt collar is damp, his face flushed.

He orders four, two shots each. She likes the little ceremony of salt and lime, the oily sting in the back of her throat. "You're on vacation, girl!" says Mickey, taking her hand, and she follows him onto the dance floor.

"I'm so glad I came!" she screams, but he can't hear her.

•   •   •   •

In Maine, in the summers, Mo bought six-packs for Mickey and his friends because she looked older. Mo worked at a jewelry store called Silver Lining and Mickey was a waiter at Lobsterman's Wharf. He made a lot in tips and had earned enough to buy a small second-hand motorboat.

On the Fourth of July they took the boat out—Mo and Mickey and a few of his friends from the restaurant. Mo bought beer for them and peach wine coolers for herself. She'd never had wine coolers before but they were lovely and sweet, like soda. The smell of peaches would always remind her of that Fourth of July.

"Mo," said Mickey. He wasn't looking at her, but up at the blue smoke where the fireworks had been. "What's up with tourists?" Mickey had just been dumped by a summer girl named Kate whose father had a Boston Whaler moored in the harbor. Her name was painted on the bow in gold cursive: "The Katherine Anne." They couldn't see the Whaler in the dark, but they knew it was there.

"Heartbreaker tourists," Mo said. Her bottle was empty and she clutched it to her belly. Kate wore tiny silver hoops in each of her four ear piercings, purchased from Mo's store.

Mickey flinched. "You," he said. His voice was sad, drunk. "You're going to be one of them."

She knew what he meant but she wanted to hear him say it. "A tourist? I live here, idiot."

"No. Heartbreaker. You're going to be a heartbreaker too."

He snorted, and his friends laughed too.

"Get your own beer, then," she said.

Amphibians

He smiled for her, secretly, a smile the friends couldn't see. As in, *I mean it.*

•   •   •   •

"My friend Abdullah has two wives," the Emirati tells Mo, nodding to the small gray-haired man across the bar. "And ten children."

"Ten." says Mo. "Wow." She hasn't had enough wine for this to seem funny.

"The first wife, she had babies, and then she had problems," he says, tapping his stomach. "And so he gets another wife." He shakes his head. He yells something across the bar and Abdullah holds up two hands with pride, fingers wiggling. "Yes, ten children, he says."

He sees Mo's expression and tries to explain.

"The husband must *ask* her. If she doesn't want him to take the second wife, she can have a divorce. So she has the choice."

Mo empties her glass. "And you have just one wife?"

"Yes, just one." He reaches for the pistachio bowl. "But I sometimes have a girlfriend." He smiles a little.

"And if your wife finds out?"

The smile disappears. "She must never know, because she will want a divorce. I have four children, and this would be no good for them. No, she must never find out."

When Mo mentions this later to Mickey—the wives, the girlfriends, the divorce procedure—he laughs. "It isn't real," he says.

"It is real. How can you laugh?"

They're at an Irish bar Mickey likes—he's on his second pint of Guinness and he looks tired. He's gazing over her head at a soccer match on TV.

She already knows what his answer will be: How can you

not laugh, Mo? Why do you have to be so fucking *serious* all the time?

She decides to speak first. "You know what Kyle said to me?" she begins.

"Who's Kyle?"

"Kyle. I told you about him. Diabetic. He dumped me."

"Oh. Yeah." He lets his eyes stray from the screen.

"He said I was a 'great girl.' I have no idea what that means."

"It means he felt bad about dumping you."

"He used the 'can we be friends' line."

"Maybe he meant it."

"He said that we weren't meant to bond physically."

"He's a monk or something?"

"No, I think it was just me."

Mickey returns to the game, not wanting to discuss this further. Someone from Manchester United kicks someone from Newcastle United hard in the shin, on purpose. The bar groans, in unison.

"Is that it?" Mo intervenes. "You have no more boy wisdom to offer?"

"I'm thinking," Mickey says, sipping his pint. "It's a tough one."

The bartender cheers for something onscreen Mo has missed and then the quarter ends with a tie. Someone yells, "Lazy frigging Geordies!"

"You just need to be more open to things. Open to people," Mickey says, scooping popcorn from a paper-lined basket.

"What does that mean, exactly, being 'open'?"

"It means being . . . friendlier. Less judgmental."

She takes this in.

"You're just too picky," he offers. "Or scared."

"Of men?" She considers this. "I haven't been tortured by you or Dad."

Christmas, she thinks. *The wrench.*

Amphibians

"Not much," says Mickey. "You just haven't had a serious boyfriend yet. I wouldn't worry about it."

"Maybe I'll meet someone here."

"That would be practical."

"Why not?"

"A drunk ex-pat. Now there's a catch."

"You're an ex-pat," she said, leaving out the drunk part.

"Not really. I'm here for a business venture." He raises his eyebrows, hinting.

You manage a bar, she thinks. "Maybe I could find a nice local guy."

"Yeah, go for it. Become wife number three."

"You said that didn't really happen."

"Of course it happens. I said it wasn't real. None of this is. The fucking fountains and the malls in the middle of the desert. The guys in their holy robes getting hammered every night. It's all made up."

"A mirage," says Mo. "The Miami of the Gulf."

"Miami? I wouldn't push it."

"So why do you stay, if it's all so fake?"

He considered this. "Because you can mess around and sleep late and do your own thing and still make decent money."

"You can do that in Maine too."

"Only in the summers," he says. "And then it gets cold as shit."

She doesn't argue.

His eyes are back on the screen and they watch together as Newcastle United loses.

"You've gone quiet," Mickey observes.

"Thinking," she says. *Come home,* she wants to say.

"You have to stop that. It isn't allowed here."

She smiles for him.

•   •   •   •

"Did you listen to the song?" the Emirati man asks.

"Yes," Mo lies. "It's beautiful, just as you said."

"I know exactly what it means now. I looked it up again. It means breast milk, for the child, the first time the mother nurses the baby." He taps his chest where a breast would be and smiles a little. "This is *lo-ra*. This is thick milk, the first milk, to protect the baby for life from the diseases. To make it healthy and strong."

"So the song is about babies?"

"No!" He shakes his head at her. "The song is about a woman. *Lura 'ayn hi Lura*. Means, 'Where is my Lura?' It is beautiful, no?"

"Beautiful." She drains her wine. This is probably not the time to tell him her real name. She's tired tonight, tired of this strange man and his song and tired of waiting for Mickey to finish work. She takes a Marlboro Light from the man's gold case without asking and strikes a match, even though he's holding out his lighter for her. It seems like she's known him for a very long time.

"Same again?" says Mickey. He winks at Mo. He's trying to get her another free drink.

"Yes, same please, Michael. Your sister, she is—" His fingers search for the right words.

Bored, thinks Mo.

"—good company," says the man. He nods, satisfied to have filled the gap.

"You should try living with her," Mickey says, cracking his smile in perfect time.

But Mo is only half-listening. She's thinking of Kyle, clearing the sheet music from his bed. *I do tantric yoga*, he'd told her. *I can go for hours.* Which had turned out not to be true at all.

Amphibians

"Excuse me," she says to the man, needing to move. She dismounts the stool as gracefully as possible.

•   •   •   •

In the Ladies' Room, a Filipina cocktail waitress is applying deodorant. "Who's the *dishdash* you sit with?" she asks. She must be new—Mo hasn't seen her before. Her smile is outlined in bright red lipstick. "Your boyfriend?" She thinks this is funny. "He must be rich."

"I don't even know him," Mo starts to explain. "I'm just on vacation."

"From Russia?" It sounds like an accusation.

"From the States. I'm American."

"Ah! American! I think you are from Russia, working here. You look Russian! So pale."

Mo holds her palms under the hand-dryer and the waitress's voice gets lost in the noise.

When Mo returns to her stool, the man is speaking to Mickey in a quiet way, leaning in.

"Must be something serious," says Mo, in her best feather-light tone.

Mickey laughs in a false way. "Business," he says.

•   •   •   •

Mickey wants to take her out again on Thursday night, the weekend. He has Fridays off. On the day of rest, he can sleep in.

Thank God It's Thursday is too crowded and so they go to the Rock Bottom Café, and the band there is *very* hard rock, all in leather. By the time they arrive the crowd is loud, reeling. Mo and Mickey drink quickly to catch up.

Later, when Mo comes back from the bathroom, her brother is kissing a short woman with a nose ring, his hands clutching her waist. But before Mo can reach them someone knocks into her, spilling beer on her sheer, blue blouse. When she looks up again, Mickey's hand is creeping along the girl's ass.

Mo gets in a cab. She has a key and Mickey won't care—he won't even remember. The driver opens his window as soon as she gets in. Does she smell? Like beer or sweat or both? On the way home, which seems to take hours, Mo watches the meter and invents a sister, pretends she's visiting her now. The sister is taller and older and very smart, a genius. She offers good advice. She isn't a bully, but she pushes Mo in a healthy way, tickles her to the point of tears on her birthday, makes her run to catch up with her on the beach.

Nose Ring, Mo considers, *is open*. And with sudden clarity she understands what Mickey means by the word.

•　　•　　•　　•

"Did you bring the lyrics?" Mo slides onto the stool, her feet dangling. The man has promised to translate her song.

The bar is busy and Mo is glad—it's her last night before flying back to Boston. There are more women than usual, beautiful women in expensive clothes with accents Mo can't quite place. They're perched next to Abdullah and Hamad and Hamaid as if they've known them a very long time. The women drink champagne and fancy cocktails. They tip back their necks and laugh.

"I forget the song! The words!" says the man.

How could you? Mo wonders. *It's all you've talked about.*

She's tipsy again, without meaning to be, but tonight she wants everything to be clear. She wants to uncover the shape of this man. Less mystery, more answers. It's the robe, it must be—it's impossible to see his outline, and this makes her want to.

His clasped hands are there, resting on the bar. Exposed.

"You like the ring?" He sees her looking. His ring is large and shiny, like the pen.

Amphibians

"I like your hands," she says.

His eyes change, flicker, everything between them shifts a little. She made the shift happen.

I'm drunk, Mo reminds herself. *I'm not myself.*

But it feels nice.

Mickey is listening, pretending not to. "How 'bout a Coke, Mo." His eyes are asking: *Want me to stop it?*

No, her eyes say. *I'm being open.*

"Busy tonight," says Mo to the man. She's careful not to look at his body.

"Yes," he says. He's smoking quickly, sucking on the end of his Marlboro for air. He seems nervous. He crushes the butt in the black enamel ashtray.

Mo's legs are crossed and her knees show, just below the hem of her skirt. He rests his fingers there, lightly, on one bare knee.

"I'd like you to come with me please," he says, leaning in.

Come where?

"I can pay you."

It takes her a second, but then she gets it.

She pulls away and looks for her brother, but he's not watching anymore. He's scrubbing glasses under the bar.

"I have to go," she says, and in the bathroom she stares at her features in the mirror until they're just that—a nose, two eyes, a smudged mouth.

He'll pay her. Russians, working here.

She feels hollow. She holds her palms under the hand-dryer and lets the warmth creep up her fingers. She shuts her eyes.

Is this why she was invited? To bump up the bar sales?

The dryer whines to a halt and she waves her palms again, she wants noise.

Her brother—what *happened* to him out here?

She finds Mickey in the storeroom, champagne bottles in his arms like bouquets.

Dishdash

"It was just a joke," he says, before she can speak.

She stares and he sets the bottles down on top of a cardboard box.

"He said he'd like to spend some time with you, and I said go ahead, ask her. But it was just a joke. Like you'd ever say yes." He smooths the flaps of his navy blue jacket. "And I only let the girls in on Saturdays, before you ask."

"Except me," she says. She isn't slurring; her words are strong, all the consonants in place. "I'm here all week."

He laughs, a little meanly. "It's not like you haven't been flirting with him."

"You fucking *pimp*."

He stops laughing. His mouth is grim, as if he's about to swear. *Cunt*, he used to say in high school, his eyes hard. But he says nothing. He picks up the bottles again, adjusts them in his arms as he leaves. They make sweet little clinking sounds like bells, like Christmas.

She waits until her heartbeat slows, until the smallest letters on the boxes become words. *Alcohol content 6% by volume. Made in the USA.*

Spring break, she thinks. *What a waste.*

And then: *He's not coming home.*

•   •   •   •

Mickey is back behind the bar, stooping down, concentrating on bottles, stacking them in neat rows behind a glass refrigerated door. He won't look at her.

The man with the song is gone.

Outside the air is heavy. There aren't any taxis.

She thinks ahead. In the morning Mickey will make coffee, like nothing has happened. He'll tell a joke and she'll laugh back, pretending to forgive him. She'll get on the plane and sleep and drink and wake up at home—cold, blurry, wanting a sweater.

Amphibians

She'll miss him. She'll call and ask about the bar, Mickey's Bar, as the regulars call it. The bar is his. It has nothing to do with her.

Headlights blind her as a Jeep slows—red, enormous, new. The glass whirs down.

"Miss Lura."

She can't see him well—he's in shadow. But the smell is his, something distinct and potent, expensive.

"Please let me apologize," he says. "I am sorry."

He's said this many times before.

"I think you are a lovely American girl and I only want to spend time with you, that is all."

That is all. Time doing what? Playing Scrabble? The thought of it makes Mo smile a little, and he mistakes this for *yes.* He clicks open the door and the bulb above his head flashes on, filling the car with light.

He looks ordinary. There are groceries on the seat beside him—a loaf of bread, a newspaper. On the floor she sees an abandoned Barbie doll. Prayer beads dangle from the rearview mirror. He lights a cigarette and offers her one.

"Thanks," she says, as briskly as possible, and takes it. "I'm not—like that." Her voice is louder than she'd intended. "I'm not like him."

"Of course not," says the man. "You are not living the fast life—living in the fast lane."

An Eagles fan. "I'm not," she agrees. "We're nothing alike." It sounds harmless, revealing it this way to this man she'll never see again.

"But you care for him, of course. He's your brother."

"I love him like a brother," she repeats. She senses the cigarette heat close to her fingers and feels incapable of moving. The Jeep door is still propped open, just room enough for her to slip in.

"Good girl," he says, shutting the door softly, and drives away.

The Mission Bell

"Any time of year, you can find it here."—The Eagles

On a dark desert highway, there's Lucy, walking. Just off the highway, there's a motel sign, pulsing red like a lighthouse. Lucy has no plan except to get there. She'll say, "My phone is dead. My Volvo is stuck three miles behind." She says this out loud, to practice.

There's wind from somewhere, light and persistent, though seconds ago it was still, just the *shht, shht* of Lucy's Birkenstocks scraping along the shoulder. She lost her elastic hair band or it's slid up her wrist to make an angry circle on her forearm. She lets the strands blow into her eyes and wishes for Joe, though they're supposed to be done. Are they done? He's in Fresno. He speaks over her—crashes into her sentences. Once he gripped her bicep and finger dots appeared the next day, a ring of proof, thrilling.

The wind dies. Her watch glows in the dark. *Who wears a watch anymore?* She slips it off, hears it smack against the roadside for someone else to find.

She thinks, *There are movies that start this way. None of them end well.*

•　　　•　　　•　　　•

In the motel doorway stands a woman smoking, the ember like

a firefly. She doesn't seem surprised to see Lucy. *You're a harmless granola and your car broke down*, says her once-over.

"My car broke down," says Lucy. "I need some gas." Her voice sounds far from her mouth.

"Already closed up shop," says the woman. "But let's see what we can do." This woman can save her, Lucy decides. Her nametag says *Tiffany*; her voice is southern. She wears her hair in a high ponytail, reddish shade. She could be 40 or 25.

The light inside is murky, like being underwater. Tiffany presses a finger against the front desk buzzer, calling whoever is in charge. She stubs out the half-burned cigarette on the sole of her high-heeled boot, clips off her nametag, slides it into her purse. A little ballet. *Do it again.*

"1H is empty and unlocked. Lazy Fuck might not bother coming down."

"Oh," says Lucy. "Let me—"

"I have to get back to my boy."

Tiffany glides out again. She unlocks her truck, reverses and plows ahead, a guitar solo leaping from her speakers. Lucy sees a flash of a glittering bumper sticker: *My Other Car Is a Mercedes.* Then it's just the drone of the muffler, receding.

Lucy waits, hopeful. But there's nothing left to see. No other vehicles in the lot.

Inside, the ceiling lamps are quiet, except for the blue light above the reception desk. *Year-round accommodation in spacious rooms*, says the tiny font on the motel pen. Lucy picks it up, wishing for a skeleton key.

She feels, for some reason, not scared. She watches three bloated, blinking goldfish. Pink light from a toy shipwreck. On the aquarium glass, a Post-it note in a child's hand. *Feed me.*

Sudden TV voices from upstairs. A laugh track.

The Lazy Fuck?

Now her heart is loud. She finds 1H, the unlocked room, a

door that feels like cardboard. She locks it from inside and falls on bedcovers, willing exhaustion. She could call Joe. But—the dead phone, back in the car. Does she hear creaking from a bed above? She smells old smoke in the pillows, which means she can light her joint without consequence. She drinks the last bottle from the minibar and lands it, empty, in the silver pail.

I fear my own boredom – what I could do to myself. She doesn't retrieve her pen and the thought disappears.

In time, her sleep is complete and holy.

In her dream, Joe reacts differently. *Of course you should have the baby.* Her parents react differently. *Of course you don't have to go back, sweet pea. Who needs a college degree?*

•   •   •   •

"Tiff!" Lucy hears at dawn. "Tiffany!" The voice is high, raspy, a child's voice. "They need more water!" Flushing, upstairs.

Lucy falls into near-sleep again. *Tiffany. A crystal chandelier. A sky-blue bag from a shop on 5th Avenue. Joe proposing with a sharp, fake ring.*

"Hello?" says a voice. Knocking, gently. "You still there?" Tiffany's voice. *The nametag.*

"You want breakfast?"

"I do." She sits up.

"Mama?" she hears, close to the door. A different child, younger.

"Shut it," says the older child. "Tiffany's working."

"But I want a piece of toast again."

Toast, thinks Lucy. *Toast and then my car.* She splashes water, smooths the covers. *I'll write a screenplay about this someday.*

The boys sit beside the toaster, the loaf of Wonder Bread, the packets of Smucker's, the empty coffee pot. They spin to stare at Lucy, unsmiling.

"Tiffany!" calls the older one. His legs swing on the barstool.

The little one's legs stick out straight. Ten and five? They wear matching black Converse sneakers and shorts. They need haircuts.

Tiffany doesn't come. A scratchy radio blares from outside. *My boy*, she said the night before. Maybe one isn't hers?

Lucy asks for two pieces of toast, please.

"I'll make it," says older.

"Ma says we should eat one piece before putting in another," says the younger.

Lucy smells herself then, a strong whiff of sourness. She wants a toothbrush.

"Do you think the manager is around?"

"Manger?" says younger.

"The man who's in charge here? I need to pay him."

"What man?"

"Oh, I thought there was a man." *The Lazy Fuck?*

Older presents the toast on a napkin. "Tiffany's in charge. Randy's gone. Red jelly? Baby Glenn ate all the purple."

Tiffany appears. "Boys! Pretty boys! Let the lady eat her toast and help me in the courtyard." She wears yellow gloves. Her nametag is gone.

"Morning," she says. "Pardon the toast. Someone forgot to do the shopping. I can order out?"

"I'm good. I should probably just pay and get my car. But I need—"

"A ride? Sure, sure. We'll get you some gas."

"Yes, I ran out of gas."

"It happens. I just need to fix this pump in the pool."

"It's just you here today? The boys said—are you the manager?"

"I do a bit of everything." Tiffany swipes at her brow. Her arms are deep tan.

"I mean, do I pay you?"

"For the toast?"

"For the room."

No one answers. The boys run ahead and Lucy follows. The pool is about the size of her car.

"Get the bucket," Tiff tells the older. He runs away and they watch him go.

"Pretty boys you have," says Lucy, echoing. *Pretty isn't right.* "Handsome."

"No, they're pretty. Glenn's father wasn't pretty but he had lashes out to here. Tiny ass. I couldn't fit into his jeans, the prick."

Lucy laughs to be polite.

"Is the pool for—"

"For use?"

Do I smell urine?

"Looks crappy, but yes, it's for swimming. Dipping. The boys like it. Frogs get in sometimes, little beasts. I'm trying to fix that. Nice summer sweat by the pool and then you dip in. We keep it cold."

"It's chlorinated?" Lucy wants more toast. Her lips are sticky with jelly. "I was a lifeguard one summer on a wicked moldy lake," she says. "Algae."

Tiffany stops to look at her.

I had to work summers, Lucy means.

"You have kids?" says Tiffany.

"I'm in college."

Tiffany's face says, *So?*

Thirst, Lucy thinks. "I was pregnant," she says. "For three months." Why is she saying this?

They stare at the leaves in the pool.

"I know how that goes," says Tiffany. "So much fucking blood. No one tells you that."

"I lost my scholarship."

Amphibians

Tiffany waits, hands on hips, sweat beading at her hairline. In the bend of her elbow, a pale slice of skin. "That sucks," she says at last.

Baby Glenn plunges his hand into the pool.

"Maybe you're lucky," says Tiff. "Kids are a trap. Aren't they, buddy?"

Lucy coughs. "Do you think I could? Some water?"

"Oh sure. You must be parched. Help yourself."

Lucy sucks from the faucet. She smears the last red packet on the bread. She listens for noises upstairs but there's nothing. On the wall there's a board filled with Post-its. *Call the Captain*, says one. *Beer and wine deliveries.*

•   •   •   •

Lucy takes a shower in 1H as Tiffany showers upstairs. She hears Tiff singing, the pipes moaning. Are they washing their hair at the same time? It might be sexy if they were.

The shampoo, Lucy smells, is just Pantene taken from a big bottle and poured into a fancy little one that says *Spirit of '69*.

She imagines, for a minute, staying right there. Ordering the deliveries. Helping to raise the boys. Letting her car rot by the side of the road.

Then it passes and she is who she is again.

•   •   •   •

"I need a smoke," Tiff says, her hair dripping on the front step.

Lucy waits. "Should I check on your boys?"

"Oh, they're fine. Livin' it up by the pool."

Lucy looks up at the unlit motel sign, remembers the Lazy Fuck. "Where did the man go?"

"What man?"

"The man you buzzed. Last night. I heard something but he never came down. He's the owner?"

"No." Tiff squints into the sun.

"Is he coming back? I should probably pay up."

"Sure. We'll just need to get you some gas."

Baby Glenn runs up from behind, padding wet feet. "I fell in!"

"Again? You need a towel?"

"I got the frogs!"

"And you didn't drown, good for you. Where's Donnie?"

"He went to find Randy."

Tiff's face shifts. She sucks her cigarette.

"Who's Randy?" says Lucy.

The boy laughs. High peels of giggles he can't stop.

"Is Randy the owner? I could leave a check if he's not around to run my card."

The boy laughs harder, his face scrunched up. He falls to the ground, laughing, his shorts soaked through.

"Randy's the ghost!" he says. "He could take your check!"

"Stop that," says Tiff. "Go get Donnie. We have to find some gas."

The boy forces out a fart. "Gas!"

Tiff laughs. "Anyway," she says to Lucy, "if you say you heard something."

"So what happened to this place?"

"What happened?"

"I mean—"

Tiffany gets up. "We need gasoline. Baby, where are those frogs?"

"In the bucket." The boy isn't laughing. "Donnie's got them. We have to stab them now?"

Tiff looks from the boy to Lucy, assessing. "Stab them? Why would you say that?"

The boy looks at his wet sneakers.

"I don't know what he means," says Tiff. "Come help me find the gas can."

75

Amphibians

Lucy looks at the boy, unsure who's being enlisted. They both follow the mother up the stairs.

Master's Chamber, says the red sign with the arrow. The carpet on the stairs is soft. Silver. Inside, the mirrored ceiling reflects the velvet bedspread.

"The honeymoon suite," says Tiff. "Excuse the mess."

But it's nearly perfect. Like it hasn't been disturbed in 40 years. There's dust on the mantel above the fireplace. The glass minibar is full, with small bottles of pink champagne in a basket. The sunken Jacuzzi, in the middle of the room, is bright red and decorated with some kind of diamond pattern inside. Until one diamond hops and Lucy looks closer and sees: an inch of water with frogs, dozens of them, slapping at one another's slick bodies, confused.

"Holy shit," says Lucy.

"I know," says Tiff. "It's disturbing. I can't think of any other place for them right now."

The boy produces a pocketknife labeled *Tool Steel*.

"You put that away, Glenn Lewis." But she doesn't sound like she means it.

"They're hard to kill, aren't they, Ma."

"No one's going to kill anything," says Tiff. She unlocks a mirrored closet door and bends to retrieve the gas can.

"Still full," she says. "This ought to get you to Fresno."

The boy peers into the hot tub, trying to count them all.

"I feel that way sometimes," says Tiff, snorting a little. "Don't you? Stuck in a fucking hole."

The boy doesn't look up as she says fucking.

"Am I a bad mother?"

"I wouldn't say that."

"Well, thanks," says Tiff.

Is she being sarcastic? The canister sloshes.

"Time for our new friend to go, Glenn," she says, and he puts the knife away, scooting to be beside them again.

"You can't!" says the boy. "You can't ever leave."

Lucy forces a laughs. "I have to. I'm so late. I'm the R.A. and I'm missing orientation. I'm supposed to be there for the freshmen. The frosh."

"But checkout isn't 'til noon," he says.

Tiff scoffs. "You don't have to check out. You never really checked in."

"Let me give you some money."

"Yes, that's fine. We just don't have to make it official."

They climb down the stairs in silence.

"Where did Donnie go?" says Glenn.

"Relax," he says, appearing from behind the counter. "I'm right here."

"You can leave the money with him," says Tiff. "I'll put this in the truck."

"But how much?"

Tiff doesn't turn. Maybe she hasn't heard. "How much?" Lucy asks the older boy.

"We'll take whatever you got," says Donnie. His eyes are glassy, like he's been programmed to say it. She looks at him. How old is he?

She leaves fifty dollars on the counter. He shoves the bills into his pocket.

"When Randy was around, we used to have big dinners here," he said. "Snails, duck, frogs' legs. I wanted Tiff to get a chandelier."

"Oh," says Lucy. She should be heading for the door. But it's hard to move.

"Do you really have to go?" says Donnie. "You just got here."

Maybe Tiff will leave without her, drive ahead to the Volvo, peer in to see the scattered Phish CDs, the unread textbooks, the plain fact of Lucy's gas gauge, three quarters full.

"I can't stay," she says. "I have to let people know where I am."

"Your family?"

"Sort of. My Joe," she whispers. "We hate each other, most of the time. But we keep each other distracted." How sick it sounds, out loud.

"Well," says Donnie, ignoring this, coming out to shake her hand. "This has been a nice surprise." He comes up to her waist. She sees that his arms are well defined. That he smells not like a child but a small, sweaty man. She shakes his palm and his grip is hard. In magic marker, on his forearm, he's written, *Alibis.*

"It's the name of my band," Donnie says, following her gaze. "I'm going to be the drummer."

"Of course," says Lucy.

Tiff honks from outside. The door is right there and Lucy feels like running for it.

"You're welcome in my home anytime," says Donnie.

His home? *The Lazy Fuck.* He lets go and she feels the damp imprint on her palm.

I will never have children, she decides.

Outside the day is boiling, hotter than the day before.

Glass

When Sam turned eight, she told her father she wanted to be a Solid Gold dancer. They were in his shop, and he said, "Sounds good, Sammy," and she loved him for this, for not laughing. They lived in Maine, which, her father reminded her, was "about as goddamned far from Solid Gold as you're likely to get." He smiled when he said this, one side of his mouth moving up like a hook. He had a fuzzy, reddish beard and eyes that drooped in a friendly way.

Sam's father was a stained glass artisan, which meant he made lamps and mirrors with fancy frames and sometimes entire stained glass windows for summer people on Ocean Point. The local craft shops sold his pieces, and he had a catalog business too, nationwide. Every November he hired an assistant to help him get through the Christmas orders.

Sam helped too. After dinner, in front of the TV, she unraveled thin strips of copper foil from a cardboard spool, narrow strips like hair, and pressed them around glass pieces her father had cut that day. The copper foil had to be wrapped tightly around the edges, and then he soldered the shapes together. The pieces looked perfect when they were first cut. Sam was sometimes tempted to swallow them whole.

Amphibians

On weekends, Sam's father took her to Ocean Point to collect mussel shells, the outsides mottled blue and the insides pearly gray and smooth against her thumb. At home she dried them in the sun on the back porch until they were bleached a dull, disappointing shade, then she wrapped these with copper too. He soldered them to things for decoration—candleholders, jewelry boxes. "Made in Maine," said the labels. The shell-pieces were his bestsellers.

There were cardboard boxes everywhere in the house, filled with shells and glass pieces and spools of copper foil. There were patterns sketched in pencil on loose-leaf paper. Dad's steel-toed boots stood by the fire like small statues. He wore thick flannel shirts. He didn't own a tie. He didn't like to dress up.

Sam's mother liked to dress up. She liked parties—New Year's, Fourth of July. For Halloween she wore old dance leotards and became a black cat or a sexy witch. For her job she wore a kind of costume too—a matching navy blue skirt and jacket with a little red scarf around her neck. The gold name-badge on her lapel was pinned exactly parallel to her left breast pocket. She was a teller at the First Federal Bank of Damariscotta, and by the time she woke Sam up for school each morning, she was already dressed and wearing pale pink lipstick.

Lately, after work, Sam's mother liked to wear loose clothes—sweatshirts and shapeless, drawstring pants. She sat in the armchair and wrapped her hands around mugs of herbal tea. She read a lot and blew at the steam, her lips pursed in a funny o.

Sam's father, after work, sat in his chair and rolled cigarettes, slowly sprinkling tobacco into little white squares and squeezing the paper between his thumb and finger. He lit the rolled tips with a candle flame and inhaled. He nodded as Sam showed him each copper-trimmed piece.

Glass

"You don't have to," Sam's mother said, blowing. She meant the glass.

"No one's forcing her," Dad said.

Sam spread out her fingers for her mother to see. She was very careful—she almost never got cuts.

But her mother wasn't looking. "What does Hart say about the state of your hands?" Mr. Hart was Sam's piano teacher.

"He prefers the Carpenters to the Bee Gees," Sam said, to change the subject.

Her father sniffed. Her mother said nothing and took her first sip of the evening. When the tea was gone she'd be allowed to have a different kind of drink.

●   ●   ●   ●

Sam's parents used to dance together. Her mother wore tight jeans and a shirt with a wide collar and her father's beard was thicker. They took disco classes at the YMCA and practiced in the living room to the *Stayin' Alive* soundtrack, tripping on the throw rug by the fire and passing a cigarette back and forth.

"You're a natural," her father had said, kissing her mother on the lips.

Sam's mother had almost been in *A Chorus Line*. She'd auditioned before Sam was born, the summer she lived in New York City alone. Two callbacks, but not a third. Sam didn't have to ask what a callback was.

They played slow songs too. "So Far Away" and "Both Sides Now." Her father held her mother very close, hardly moving at all, and she smiled in a distracted way, her head resting on his flannel shoulder.

When they stopped taking lessons, Sam thought it had something to do with the Death to Disco sticker she'd seen in town, on a Saab with New York plates. When she was alone in the house, Sam sometimes pulled the records from their sleeves one by one, to look for nicks.

Her mother danced on her own sometimes, when her father was out. There was no music. She scooted around the living room with a Bloody Mary, with coiled urgency. It seemed private.

Sam wanted to move like that, with ease or with purpose. She wanted her mother to teach her how.

•   •   •   •

In ballet class, Sam wasn't allowed to wear her Bee Gees t-shirt. She had to wear pink tights and a black leotard, just like everyone else. She liked the scratchy old piano records. She liked to watch the other feet and pretend they weren't connected to other girls. Just feet. She tried to explain but Ms. Dardonne, the ballet teacher, said, "Chin up. No cheating."

Near the end of class, Ms. Dardonne pushed the bar to the side of the room. It made a terrible screeching sound, like wheels braking. The other girls lined up in groups of three, no talking allowed. Sam followed.

Ms. Dardonne said, "S*tep, step LEAP, step, step LEAP!*" She said it over and over, and still Sam had to think very hard about what to do. She thought, *left, left,* and out of nowhere her right leg appeared, flinging itself out. Her stomach turned. *What was wrong with her?* She knew the steps. But the other bodies—they confused her. They pulled her away from her own thoughts. She wanted the bar, the cool solid roundness underneath, the way it made her palm smell nice, like sweet, salty rust.

Her mother, after lessons, asked to see what Sam had learned. Sam tried hard to remember, standing in the living room, still in her leotard. Her father was there and he pretended not to, but he was watching, and Sam liked that too. Her mother told her to push her shoulders back and hold her arms in an arc, as though she was hugging a giant ball. Arms were very important. "Make them strong," said her mother. "Then people won't notice your feet so much."

Ms. Dardonne thought Sam might be dyslexic.

"That's ridiculous," said Sam's mother. "You're just not concentrating."

They began to practice before Dad came in, on days when Sam didn't have classes. Mom sipped her Bloody Mary and put on very old records, classical music, and she taught Sam routines she remembered. She taught Sam to make an L with her thumb and forefinger.

"See? L for left." And Sam would make the L automatically, for the rest of her life, whenever anyone asked her for directions.

Sam wasn't dyslexic after all. She was glad, she supposed, but it was a little disappointing. It would have been nice to have a reason.

•   •   •   •

In October, Dad's workdays were longer. His boots dragged against the worn floorboards of the shop. On weekends, Sam wrapped at his worktable and felt the tremors of his steps.

He kept the radio on all day as he drew and cut his patterns. He liked the Eagles and the Steve Miller Band and Jackson Browne. He liked Stevie Nicks but he didn't like Blondie or Pat Benatar.

On his worktable, he kept a notebook, a straightedge ruler, a compass, and a coffee mug of yellow #2 pencils, the erasers nibbled, like a squirrel had been there. He drew and chewed and Sam watched him until he forgot she was there.

A space heater kept the shop warm and three big lamps hung from the ceiling like umbrellas. There was a hot plate and a kettle, for tea breaks, and an old torn couch in the corner. There were metal shelves stacked high with her father's tools: pattern shears and breaking pliers, X-Acto knives and glass-grinders. There were soldering irons and burnishers to meld the copper foil, and wooden jigs, like frames, for holding the glass pieces together. There was one jagged hacksaw that Sam wasn't allowed to touch.

"DAD."

He looked up, surfacing. He asked if she was bored yet and she said no, not really, and he said didn't she want to play outside? Swing? Hunt for acorns? She said she was too old for that. She kept wrapping.

In November, her father hired a girl named Sharon McDougal, who lived just a few miles away on Red Pine Road. Sharon had been a student at the Portland College of Art and was Dad's helper for the season, or apprentice, as she called herself.

"She's slow," said Sam.

"She's learning," said Dad.

Sharon came to the shop on Saturday afternoons wearing thick wool sweaters patterned in purples and blues. She tied back her long hair with a pewter barrette shaped like a scallop. Her wedding ring had a tiny diamond. She'd married a lobsterman, Sam's father said, when she was just eighteen. The lobsterman's name was Brady and he was a loud, friendly sort with long hair and a boat called 'The Sharon Louise.' On weekends, Brady went diving for sea urchins, which was very hard work for good money, because urchins were a delicacy in Japan.

One time, diving, Brady got caught. (Sam's father cleared his throat.) A buoy line, he said.

Sam wanted more, but her father wouldn't say. Brady had gone diving, and he died. It was a very dangerous job to have.

Sharon had moved away and tried art school, but she came back after a year. She hadn't cared much for Portland, she told Sam's father.

Late one afternoon, the heater churning, Sam sneaked up

behind and snapped the clasp of Sharon's barrette and watched Sharon's hair fall to her waist.

Sharon whirled around, her loose strands black and soft -looking. "Quit it, Sammy." Her face was worried.

"You—*widow*," said Sam, trying out the word.

Sam spent the rest of the afternoon in the woods behind the house. She'd meant to say: *Only Dad calls me that.*

•   •   •   •

On Thanksgiving weekend, Dad's truck, parked along the shore-side, was the only car on Ocean Point Road. Sam sat in the truck's cab next to her father with the heat on, rubbing her hands together. The tide was coming in and her father stared; gray waves lapped at the seaweed, covering up the tidal pools. The sun was distant and Arctic looking, a frozen yellow smudge. Rainwater dripped from Sam's red poncho and made the seat damp. Her fingers were gritty with sand.

"Slim pickings today," her father said. He reached across the cab for his tobacco in the glove compartment.

Sam held a blue Tupperware container in her lap. The lid had been lost, so her mother let them use it for shells. Today they had ten good mussels, five periwinkles, two razor clams, one dried-out sea urchin and a black rock with a white ring around it. The rock couldn't be soldered, but her father said she should make a wish and throw it out to sea. Like birthday wishes, he said, like throwing pennies in the fountain at the Portland Mall.

Dumb, Sam thought. *They never come true.*

They were parked across the street from the old stone chapel. It was boarded up now, but from May to September there were weddings there every weekend, mostly for summer people. It was a tiny church, with a single stained glass porthole above the door.

Sam pointed. "Who made that window?"

"I'm not sure," he said. Her father smoked and stared at the waves. After a while he said, "Your mother wanted to get married there, but it was pricey."

"How old were you?"

He looked up, surprised by the question.

"Pretty young."

"As young as Sharon and Brady were?"

He looked down at his fingers, his knuckles red. "Almost." He placed more tobacco in the center of another white square.

Sam waited for him to lick the cigarette shut, then asked, "When Brady drowned, did you go to the funeral?"

"No, I didn't know Sharon then."

"Sharon should've stayed in school. Mom said."

"Did she now." He struck a match.

"Sharon could be an art teacher that way. But then she wouldn't work for you."

"No," her father said. He recognized Davey Johnson's blue Ford Fiesta in the rearview mirror and jerked his head up in greeting. The heat was on full blast now. Sam held her hands in front of the vent.

"Warming up?" he said.

Sam nodded. She didn't want to leave.

Her father rolled down the window an inch and flicked out the cigarette, then revved the truck's old engine. The lobster buoys bobbed, their white stems all tipped at the same angle, like dancers in a line.

•　　　•　　　•　　　•

Sam took ballet on Tuesdays and Thursdays and piano lessons on Fridays. Mr. Hart lived just five houses down the road, but Sam liked to pretend it was much further away, and that crazy people lurked in ditches with axes, people she'd have to fight off.

Mr. Hart had very long fingers and lived alone, except for his

Siamese cat, Brava. He made Sam a cup of cocoa and showed her photo albums from when he'd lived in New York and Paris and Berlin. He was thinner in these pictures, and handsome. He was Ms. Dardonne's friend—there were pictures of them together, sipping cocktails at Fisherman's Wharf.

The piano took up Mr. Hart's entire living room. In his kitchen, Mr. Hart had a shelf filled with porcelain figurines. Sam's favorite was a mermaid holding a marble-sized crystal ball in her tiny white hands.

"You'll get it," said Mr. Hart. He meant "Let It Be," which was harder than it sounded. He closed the book and let her take it home. They were ending the lesson early. He had a date with Ms. Dardonne.

Sam walked home as slowly as possible, placing her heel exactly in front of her toe. She held the Beatles book against her chest, careful not to bend the pages. The sky was losing light and the ground was slick with dead, brown leaves. There were slugs underneath, she imagined, orange and fat. The birch trees were bare. It would be nice to peel off the bark in thin white sheets, but it wasn't good for the tree.

She'd have plenty of glass to wrap, with Christmas coming soon. Even her mother had been helping out, letting her tea go cold.

She passed the Kensey's house and counted twenty-two lobster traps stacked on the front lawn. Mrs. Kensey would place a single white candle in each window. Sam's mother would make wreathes from snapped spruce boughs and Dad would put one on the shop door. Her mother made blackberry jam at Christmas too, from berries she'd frozen. Maybe she'd made some already. Maybe she and Dad would be in the kitchen when she got home, lips sticky, crumbs on the table.

Sam walked around back first, to the shop. Red pieces today, probably—they'd finished all the green. The pine door was swollen and damp and she had to push hard with her shoulder to open it. The lights were out but the space heater was on, casting an orange shadow on the floorboards. It was very quiet. Something moved in the corner, near the couch. "Dad?" She saw the outline of her father's boots near the heater and something fuzzy and soft on the worktable, a sweater.

"Sam. Go back in the house." Dad's voice was cool, stern. Sam didn't move, didn't even exhale.

"Get out, Sam. *Now.*"

She ran, her feet heavy. She dropped the Beatles book and picked it up, brushing away damp leaves. Outside everything was in shadow, except one thick streak of sky, all fiery and rust-colored, huge and angry and much too far away.

•　　　•　　　•　　　•

Years later, when Sam thought of that day, she pictured Sharon and her father on the kitchen table, jam on Sharon's lips and Dad's hands clutching at her. There was jam everywhere, everything sticky.

At the time, she had a sharp feeling in her gut, like glass inside. She tried hard to imagine nothing. She said nothing.

Her mother found out anyway. From her room Sam heard a short laugh like a bark, like something was caught in her mother's throat. Then her father slammed doors (house, porch, pick-up). He didn't go anywhere, just sat in the truck smoking for an hour, then two, flicking out the rolled butts until there was a little pile under the driver's window.

A week later, her mother put her vanity case and a duffel bag in the back of the old Subaru and drove all the way to Key West, where the highway stopped. She worked at a bar called Lucky's where she had to wear a purple tank top, she wrote. She sent postcards of pelicans, of Ernest Hemingway's house. Her bank uniform hung in the closet, pressed and starched.

Glass

Sam stayed in her room and traced her finger along I-95 in her father's atlas, Maine to Florida. It was nothing, just three finger-lengths down the page.

Sharon was gone. She went back to school. This is what Allie Thompson told Sam. Allie was Sam's best friend, and Allie's mother got her hair cut by Sharon's mother, and this is what Mrs. Thompson heard during her tri-monthly perm and set.

•   •   •   •

By March, the birch trees had tiny buds and Sam's shoes were muddy. Her mother called and asked if she'd like to spend the summer in Florida. Her voice sounded different, the tightness in her throat gone. She sounded tan and pretty.

"I have my lessons," said Sam. "My recital." *Come get me*, she thought. She felt a tug like a rope tightening.

Sam practiced the Beatles songs in her room, on the paper keyboard on the back cover of the Young Adult Piano Book #1. She tried to hear the notes in her head and sometimes this kept her from hearing the TV downstairs and her father coughing in front of it. She made up songs of her own. She did pliés in front of the mirror, in her tiara. She was too old for the tiara, but she wanted to wear it still.

She thought of Sharon's finger, on the left hand, with the tiny diamond.

She thought of Key West as a steep green cliff and her mother standing too close to the edge.

She practiced.

•   •   •   •

In the fall, Sam was allowed to start jazz classes at the Brunswick Y, forty minutes away, and by the time they got back to town the roads were black and empty. Dad drove fast, with the stereo on, the window wide open. He smoked and didn't sing. He'd stopped

89

rolling cigarettes. He bought Marlboro Reds instead.

Sam was the youngest one in the class. Ms. Lynn, the teacher, said, "You have grace. It's a gift."

"It's from my mother," said Sam, and handed over the checks.

Ms. Lynn wanted Sam to take a modern class, too, but her father wouldn't budge.

He spent more time in the shop, alone. The house smelled musty, like wet leaves. Sam lit all the candles at once: Apple Cinnamon, Vanilla Musk, Lilac Breeze. She watched them burn and puddle, waiting for her tea to cool.

●　　　●　　　●　　　●

For Halloween, Sam was John and Allie was Paul. Allie took lessons from Mr. Hart too. She was already on Book #3 and she had a two octave Casio to practice on, with drumbeats: salsa, march, waltz and rock. She wanted Sam to spend the monthly checks on 45's, but Sam wouldn't. Allie had a big 45 collection already, alphabetized by artist.

Sam's mom sent a postcard of a Carnival ship, docked in Miami. She said she'd been on a mini-cruise to the Bahamas, with a friend. The ship was very large, like a perfect tooth. The dancers wore feathers and rhinestone earrings, she wrote.

Sam would never work in a bank or a bar, she decided, and she wouldn't sit in a dark shop and make things all day. Solid Gold had gone off the air, but she had a new plan. She would be a Radio City Rockette. She would have to be five-foot-five, at least. Allie was the only one she told.

"You probably won't be tall enough," Allie said.

Allie was going to be a keyboard player for Prince.

"He plays the piano himself," Sam pointed out.

"I'll do it for him. He'll be free to sing and dance that way."

They would be famous, this was certain. They just had to get out.

Glass

Her mother flew back to Maine for a visit, after Thanksgiving. She took Sam to the Tugboat Inn and ordered ginger ales for both of them. Her hair was shorter and she wore a bracelet with small coral hearts. She asked about Sam's dance classes and showed pictures from her Bahamas trip.

Sam slid her orange garnish from the side of her glass and chewed. "You know the *Chorus Line* story?" Her heart rattled but she couldn't stop herself. "It sounds made up."

"It's not made up," said Sam's mother. She sucked the last of her ginger ale.

In the harbor the water was steely and quiet. No waves. Sam waited, but her mother just smiled hard. Then she asked for the bill.

•   •   •   •

The piano recital was a week before Christmas and Sam only made one flub. Ms. Dardonne came and sat in the front row. Her father came and clapped too much. Allie went last and played "Long and Winding Road."

Sam began to have the same dream. The ship's funnel was spewing brown leaves, thousands of them, so many that the green Astroturf of the deck was covered, and stems were caught in the plastic slats of sun chairs. Sam knew the shape of the leaves but couldn't remember the tree name. And she knew her father was there—underneath somewhere, hiding.

Her mother was there too, standing at the ship's rail with her new haircut ruffled. The leaves swirled around her and the sea churned below, and her mother just kept standing there on deck, as if she'd taken root. She clenched something in her fist. And when she saw Sam, she sprung into action, beautifully. She twirled and arched, and flung back her rigid arm like a pitcher, like an expert. She threw just as far as she could.

Belly Dancing

United Arab Emirates: Month One, 1999

Allie's a little embarrassed, watching the veils, and so are the other women in the bar—the ex-pat wives from England, India, and Australia. They either brace their lips in a smile, clapping too hard—*Look, I'm not intimidated by a half-naked woman gyrating in the presence of my husband*—or they ignore the belly dancer altogether. Allie opts for the smile grimace, her work expression. She feels it's her duty as a fellow entertainer. She knows it's better to be watched than ignored.

Tonight is "Arabic Night" in the five-star hotel bar where Allie works as a cocktail pianist. She gets a break tonight, two sets instead of four. She helps herself to the buffet (kebabs, falafel, hummus) and watches the belly dancer do her thing. It's a little weird: Arabic Night in Dubai, like American Night in Boston. But the veils and bellies are rare now. Dubai, it seems to Allie, has traded the dancers for shopping malls. There are rules about drinking and showing too much skin, yet there are just as many hotel bars as mosques, and miniskirts for sale at the Al Jazeera Fashion Plaza. The guidebooks don't help Allie here. There is much she doesn't understand.

Amphibians

The food and beverage manager, Nadia, catches Allie's eye and puffs out her cheeks like Dizzy Gillespie. "*Fat*," she says, sitting next to Allie at the bar. She means the roll of skin above the dancer's tight harem pants.

Nadia has worked in the hotel for nine years. She's Lebanese but went to school in London and has a slight cockney accent. She tells Allie how much the belly dancer makes for twenty minutes of dancing. It's more than Allie makes per day.

Allie isn't sure why Nadia is telling her this.

"At least this one is Arab," Nadia continues.

The last dancer was Russian, and all the locals complained that she was too pale. Her legs jerked ahead of the beat as her stomach did its thing. She smelled like sweat. Though she did have chutzpah, grand entrances, big poses.

The new belly dancer, the Arab one, has better technique, but it takes her a while to get into it. During the first song she seems self-conscious, not because of what she's doing, but because her entrance hasn't been properly recognized. She's up to her neck in gauze and yet the guests are still absorbed in their baklava and coffee with their backs to her. She keeps playing with her hair, fluffing it forward to cover her displeasure. She signals accusingly to her keyboard player—*Speed it up*—making it his fault. It's instinct to do this, Allie knows.

But the dancer soon recovers. Her jaw unclenches, and her belly becomes her own. She shimmies to the bar, twirling in Allie's direction with her eyes lowered. She's dancing in a way that means Allie should copy her.

Again, Ally feels her face congeal, her expression taxed: attempted good cheer. It's important to look like a good sport in front of the guests. So Allie shimmies back.

Nadia pats her on the thigh. Approval. Allie has passed the shimmy test.

The dancer winks a kohl-lined lid and moves on.

Belly Dancing

• • • •

Humaid, a local, is a regular in the lobby bar during Allie's cocktail sets. His robe is white. He wraps his Heineken bottle in a candy-red napkin, label hidden. He has a small circuit of bars in Dubai where he's permitted to sit and get slowly stoned.

It's several days after Arabic Night, and Humaid says the belly dancer's name is Maha, which means, "white gazelle with big eyes." It's a very rare animal, and Humaid has seen only one in his lifetime, "in the dunes of the Empty Quarter." Allie understands this to mean *in the Dubai Zoo*. She listens to Humaid six nights per week.

Humaid says he knows Maha from her other gig, her posh gig in an actual nightclub where she's the main attraction, not just decor for the buffet. "I stared like this," he says, demonstrating, not slack-jawed like a cartoon but with chin in hand and eyes narrowed. Rapt.

• • • •

Allie imagines she hasn't changed since college, that she's still a bra-less skinny-dipper, although it's impossible to be either in Dubai. The truth is, she's unnerved here—all this slobbering over bare skin with the wives at home in their veils.

She tried to explain to her mother on the phone last week, about the grocery store, how the butcher points at her legs if she wears shorts.

"Shouldn't you cover up?" her mother suggested. "Respect the local culture?"

She was right, of course, but it wasn't what Allie wanted to hear.

In Shanghai a little girl had tried to touch Allie's eyelashes. They'd seemed so long to her. In Osaka, a grizzled man had followed her around for an hour only to ask, when Allie

Amphibians

whirled around to confront him, "Practice English, please?" But in Dubai the staring is different. Allie feels a pleasant flush at first, then something else. Distant panic. As if, at the root, she's a disappointment and they'll soon find out. She won't be able to convince them otherwise.

There is another example, which Allie doesn't share with her mother: An Emirati man, smelling of whiskey, followed her into the elevator. He showed Allie his room key with 203 imprinted on brass. She assumed that he couldn't see the numbers or perhaps couldn't read them because they weren't in Arabic numerals, so she smiled and pressed 2.

When the door opened, he made a little flourish with his hand. She shook her head and smiled. "It's not my floor."

He flourished again. She refused again.

He frowned and dangled the key.

"No," she said, not smiling. He left.

It scares her—not the prevalence of horny men and prostitutes—but her reaction to them, the sudden instinct not to smile, not to engage. This new rule with male strangers: *Don't let your eyes meet theirs.*

●   ●   ●   ●

Humaid, no longer a stranger, is still deep in thought, deep into Maha. "This girl, such a talent," he says. "I just couldn't stop myself from watching her." He drains his beer, and Allie excuses herself. Her break is over.

But it takes three songs before she can focus. She hears her ninth-grade piano teacher: *Audiences are like dogs. They can smell the fear.*

This isn't stage fright, singing to Humaid in a lobby lounge.

This is the fear that no one will ever see her as they see Maha, with eyes instead of teeth. With genuine interest as opposed to buzzed curiosity.

Belly Dancing

•   •   •   •

Maha the belly dancer, Allie imagines, at home in her very own nightclub, has a brilliant male accompanist in a glittering zebra-striped vest. He shouts in Arabic and pounds the keyboard with his fists. There's a ridiculous cover charge, nearly one hundred American dollars. It's dark inside. The white robes of the locals are muted. They sit on cushions or in elaborate settees, close to the ground.

The dancer does her show. Not for long—twenty minutes, half an hour, tops. She needs her rest. Her steps have been tightly rehearsed. She has a dozen routines and varies them to keep herself amused. She has thirty-one separate costumes, worth thousands of *dirhams* each. If a regular happens to come into the nightclub every night for one month, he has to wait thirty-one days before he sees the same outfit again. The costumes have to be sent out for repairs and washing. She had a Filipino dry cleaner fired for damaging the sequins.

There are no catcalls or whistles as she dances, only loud, flat-palmed clapping—either steady on the beat or rapid eighth notes—which makes the men's palms sting. When they aren't clapping, they're clutching squat glasses with ice and whisky. Bottles appear from behind the bar with family names engraved on silver tags. A waiter stands at the side, waiting to bend and refill, bend and refill.

The belly dancer gets tips, mostly bottles of Moët. She tells the bartender not to open them, so he fills a champagne flute with ginger ale instead. She takes only one tiny sip, toasting the tipper across the room, her jewelry tinkling. She isn't expected to sit with the tippers. They would be baffled if she did.

How odd it must have been to find herself in Allie's lobby bar for Arabic Night, where anyone could have reached out to

Amphibians

touch her veils, her arms. She was just a party trick there. Why would Maha need to do such a thing?

Month Two

On her day off, Monday, Allie finally looks up *habibi* in Book Corner, which is located in Citi Center Mall. She knows that she could ask Humaid or any other Emirati for a literal definition—the men say it constantly—but she likes to look things up. She appreciates the neat order of words listed, alphabetized and explained.

This particular dictionary, thin with gray paper and miniscule print, is not expansive. "Love; my dear," it says, and that's all. Something a cashier might say in England: *Two pound eighty, love.* Allie was hoping for something juicy, like woman, wife, and whore all rolled together into one. Something to fling back at the next man in the elevator, if only in her head.

Why can't she just laugh instead? Why can't she maintain a sense of humor in the face of bizarre *Lonely Planet* encounters?

Allie plans her route: Ikea to Woolworths to Baskin Robbins. A good three hours eaten up, maybe four if she dawdles. Then a movie. *I like malls,* she tells herself. She likes that she can be alone here without feeling antisocial.

She walks past Woolworths without going in. She buys her cone—one scoop of Rocky Road—and eats it quickly. She purchases her ticket much too early and waits to sneak the can of Heineken from her purse once the lights fade. The movie is heavily edited. When Kevin Spacey leans in to kiss young Mena Suvari, a full second of blackness chops the scene in two.

I don't have any friends yet, Allie understands in the cool dark. Only acquaintances who work odd hours, like her. She knows the lead singer from the band in the Hard Rock Café— the one from Glasgow who chain-smokes. She knows a few of the Emirates Air flight attendants from the hotel gym, tall, tan and chipper. She knows them well enough to chat in the changing room, and most of the time that's sufficient. She doesn't crave their friendship, although the fact that she doesn't crave it worries her sometimes.

I know Mary Anne, she reminds herself, the American who drinks in the lobby bar, with big nuggets of silver and stone hanging from her dainty ears and wrists. She was married to a man from Yemen for a while, and says 'ex-husband' quickly, to get her mouth around the word.

I'm paid to listen. To Mary Anne and Humaid and everyone else. She shouldn't mind. It's small talk. Her cheeks ached in the lobby lounge, her smile stuck again, when Nadia suggested she wear shorter skirts to show off her legs, when Humaid slipped out with a heavily made-up Russian woman and returned later, alone, to show Allie recent pictures of his ten grandchildren. When an Egyptian guest cringed at the mention of Israel. ("I don't know this place," he said. "I know only Palestine.") When Mary Anne said she could pee standing up. She'd wanted to be like her brothers, so she'd practiced in the shower for years.

On those nights, Allie drank more. She felt not quite sane, with so many opinions rattling around inside.

She likes to argue. She's good at it.

"Sometimes it's best to accept things," Allie's father had often said. She'd told on Dee Dee Winters when she said faggot during recess, and then told again when Dee Dee chased her home from school.

"It's best sometimes to keep quiet," said her father. Dee Dee's father, Mr. Winters, was his client. "Choose your battles."

Or else what? She'll be alone?

She thinks of pre-pubescent Mary Anne, peeing in the shower, aiming for the drain.

Amphibians

She thinks of Dee Dee Winters. "I'm getting out of here," Allie had told Dee Dee from the top of the monkey bars. "You'll be stuck here your whole damn life."

The joy of travel is the joy of reinventing yourself, abandoning all that you were before. But maybe it isn't healthy to live like this, so buoyant, so far from people who tell her who she really is.

The lights come up. She has no idea what the movie was about. Beauty? Pervy Americans? She pushes the empty can deep into her purse.

Two months down. Four left to go, with the option to renew for an additional three.

●   ●   ●   ●

Again, in the gym. A flight attendant tells Allie a story: Her co-worker was living with an Emirati. The co-worker did a fly-over to Sydney and returned to find him dead on the kitchen floor. The police said it must have been a heart attack, took the body away, then put the girlfriend in jail for three days—not as a suspect but for cohabiting with a man out of wedlock.

"I swear to God, it's true," the flight attendant says, sucking from her water bottle. "She's out now, of course, but can you imagine?"

They're biking stationary, side-by-side, and Allie slows her pace, politely, to take it in. Yes, she can imagine. She feels nothing. Just a desire to be alone in the shower, clean. "Excuse me," she says, and goes there.

●   ●   ●   ●

Scott Barter was Allie's reason for sticking with the piano, after Mr. Hart retired. Her other option, or so she believed in high school, was to become an anchorwoman for the Portland news channel. Scott had a dozen or so private students, all budding flutists and sax players, except for Allie, his only advanced musician and his only pianist. No one had called her a musician before.

Scott had permission from the high school to use the band room in the evenings after he finished his job waiting tables at the Thistle Inn. He wasn't married. He devoted his time to music: listening, practicing, teaching. He played four instruments and had just graduated from the Portland Conservatory.

"Too young to know anything about teaching, if you ask me," her father said, giving her the money.

Scott lent her *In the Dark*, and she listened to it in bed every night, beginning to end. When Jerry Garcia died a few months later, she cried. Scott cried too. He said she could keep the CD.

He brought new CDs each time, and then an adapter with two headphone jacks so that they could listen together on his Discman. They spent the entire hour like that, almost touching, side by side on the piano bench. Allie liked that they were deaf to each other, deaf to everything but the music blaring.

After they started having sex, he wouldn't let Allie pay for lessons. So she kept the money from her father. She bought CDs and Dove Bars and spermicidal jelly. They locked the band room door and turned off the lights. They unlocked the closet and tried on the marching band uniforms, naked underneath, shiny brass buttons and his lips on her neck and along her spine. The janitor said nothing.

Her parents noticed she wasn't practicing. Her mother dusted the piano daily with an old brown washcloth.

I'm advanced, she thought, although they hadn't said a word.

When Scott left town for a four-month ferry gig—Portland to Halifax and back—Allie felt a sharp ache in her throat. She practiced for distraction. She transposed all of *In the Dark* into keys she could sing and then moved on to *Court and Spark*.

Amphibians

When Scott came back from the ferry —twenty pounds heavier and quite pale—Allie's ache was gone, and she knew sixty-three pop songs by heart.

Month Three

From the balcony of her Dubai apartment in hot, muggy April, Allie watches a man in a pale blue dress—a *kurta*, she's been told—in the parking lot below. He's busy wiping cars clean of sand and dust that will land again tomorrow. It's a big lot and it will take him hours to do this, if he finishes at all—so many Jeep Cherokees and Jags and Mercedes. *Inshallah*, God-willing, Allie hears him mutter from time to time. But she can also see, in the resigned stoop of his spine, a lack of resentment about this task.

She thinks again, *I don't truly know anyone here.*

It occurs to her that playing cover tunes is similar. She spaces out sometimes, suddenly on verse three. (Had she played verse two?) She doesn't improvise because the guests don't like it. They like to hear the radio versions, as close to the original as possible. They clap, most of the time, because the silence between the songs makes them nervous.

She only has to work four hours a day. In eight years she's lived in twelve countries. She's twenty-eight years old, which is not old.

She thinks of Scott, still home, still waiting tables at the Thistle between ferry jobs.

Allie wonders if she should have stayed in music school, stuck it out past sophomore year. She'd liked Boston, the severity of all that red brick. The relative distance from Maine. The school practice rooms were cigarette-pocked and smelled like feet but Allie locked herself in for hours at a time, feeling tight and focused. There were few women there. Occasionally she caught a man looking through the porthole window of the room—a fellow pianist clutching sheet music by Bach or Keith Jarrett or Joe Jackson—not watching her hands, not waiting for the room, but directing a zoo-stare at a species out of place. She learned to cover the pane with her wool scarf.

She worked part-time at Tower Records on Newbury Street for the discount and played shitty gigs on the weekends with a band she joined for the name alone, *Spark Court.* She lugged her keyboard up many flights of stairs, played for beer and tips, then packed it up and lugged it all back down.

But some nights with the band it all came together, and those times were worth the schlep. It could have been too much beer or not enough sleep, but it was like she was speaking without having to explain herself. She wasn't arguing, just speaking.

Then she saw the ad in the *Phoenix* for a five-star hotel residency in the south of France. How perfect that seemed to her in her frigid Somerville room: a baby grand in a shiny marble lobby. The ad said, "all found," meaning room and board and flight included. *All found.* She liked the sound of it. She called the number and skipped her midterms and began packing.

Now Allie looks down at the cars in the dusty lot and exhales slowly, counting to five, knowing she has coffee breath. She checks the interval between the disparate sound of air conditioning units: minor third. The balcony ledge is white with dust. She's careful not to let her sleeves touch.

She'd been reading in the window seat last time she was home. Her father had called out from another room, just her name, but clearly a summons.

He was in the kitchen, reading from the *Portland Press Herald* with the pages spread out like a map. "Up and coming," he read aloud. It was something about the music scene in Portland.

There was a clipping too, a classified ad, circled in red pen. "Music Teacher Wanted, Lincoln County School District." Seeing it, Allie had two impulses: hug her father tight and run far away.

Allie drags herself from the balcony, puts on lipstick. She has twenty minutes before the bus arrives for work.

She cuts through the parking lot, loose sand in her high heels. The dustman is hidden in the shadows, probably resting behind one of the Jeeps.

She lets herself be lured by the flashing neon lights of Pic 'n Save, where there is little for Allie to buy, just Arabic newspapers and six-packs of Sprite, on sale because the cans are past their expiration dates. Metal hooks dangle above the butcher's counter with a sign that says "Pork Shop. Not for Muslims." Allie lingers in front of the counter, looking at the meat, the reds and pinks and labeled parts: "shoulder," "rib," "tongue." Her butcher isn't there—the one who points at her bare legs—so she leaves.

When the bus arrives outside Allie's building, she climbs in and folds herself into the only spare seat, next to a Filipina waitress who smiles and nods. Allie smiles back and that's it. As the bus pulls up to the staff entrance, Allie peers around and tries to place the rest of the faces. They're all familiar by now—cleaners, security officers, wait and bar staff; the technician that fixed Allie's microphone lead and the receptionist from the gym. They all know her name, calling her Miss Allie or A-*lee*, but she doesn't know their names, not one.

Month Six

Allie loses a rhinestone earring before work. She slaps her palm to the floor, searches under the bed until she feels something glassy. She catches her reflection in the mirror—panic, subdued. But it's not just her face. It's the dress and the padded bra. It *looks* padded. She'd never noticed. Had anyone else? The bar staff? Why hadn't they told her?

Belly Dancing

She doesn't know what she looks like anymore. She knows how to reflect, how to become what they want to see.

Big breaths. She pokes the earring post in her lobe and locks it into place.

She's running out of time in the UAE. An option: She'll get an apartment in Boston, her own place. She has enough money saved. She'll wear funky clothes from second-hand stores instead of low-cut slinky dresses. She'll make chili for her girlfriends on weekends, drinking wine while chopping onions. They'll laugh and confess, and then burn all padded things in a ceremonial way. She doesn't yet know who these girlfriends will be.

She has started drinking before work. Just one glass of wine at the bar prior to her first set and maybe one more during her first break. Mary Anne or Humaid will buy one or two later in payment for their requests. She has a nightcap as well, to wind down, and feels better by the time she gets home.

In bed she has the same fuzzy epiphany and then forgets. It has to do with something her mother had said last time, something new.

"You'd better learn to *live* on that pedestal of yours."

Her repertoire is expanding, she'd thought. But it stuck.

The pedestal she imagines is a shiny black leather piano stool, and as it circles round and round at a dizzying speed it gets taller and taller, like a barber's chair. It squeaks a little. She can only come back down if someone far below steps on the pedal, with all their weight. Then she'll descend without a sound.

●　　　●　　　●　　　●

It's her day off again, so Allie has more time than usual for Pic 'N Save. There's not a lot she wants to photograph in Dubai, but the pork sign is funny. She knows she should probably ask first, but instead—after working up her nerve—she stands behind a shelf of sliced bread, frames the sign, and waits for a veiled woman to pass by with her trolley.

The butcher, Allie's butcher, hears the click of the camera and marches over. He's small with curly hair, like John Oates from Hall and Oates. There's blood on his apron, maybe on his hands too.

He grabs her arm just above the elbow, where her shirtsleeve stops. "Not allowed," he says. "You must give me the camera." His eyes are tired looking.

Allie's tempted to laugh. She realizes how ridiculous she must look, but she knows better. She adopts a confused expression and says, "Sorry, I didn't know."

"Americans," he says. His breath smells of something sweet and delicious, like baked apples or fried dough. "You."

His hand is still squeezing her bicep, with one stubby thumb digging in with more pressure than necessary. It hurts just enough to keep her still.

He's waiting for something. An apology? A phone number?

She smiles weakly, to fill the silence.

He smiles back, then lets go. She wants to rub her arm but doesn't.

He touches his scalp, scratching distractedly. He's chewing on something. Candy or his cheek? He looks around. The veiled woman is gone, leaving the aisle empty. He changes his mind and reaches out again.

Allie steps back, bumping against the bread shelf. "Don't fucking touch me!"

Her heart thumps. Why did she say "fucking"? He could call the police. He could get her thrown in jail like the stewardess. She'd have to live in a small cramped space with urine-stained sand on the floor, her skin touching other people's skin for hours at a time.

"Touch you?" he says. He wipes his hands on his apron. His

face says, *Why would I want to do that?*

Allie pushes open the glass doors. The heat washes over her. She's crying, so she stops in the middle of the sidewalk and pretends to lock shut her purse. A Jeep slows and pauses. An invisible driver watches behind tinted windows, then moves on.

There are no Emirati butchers. The locals aren't permitted to perform such menial tasks, of course not. He's Syrian, maybe, or Lebanese. He won't report her or track her down. He won't ever try to find her.

She walks home. *Nothing will happen*, she understands, and feels more regret than she can explain.

•   •   •   •

"I'm going, I think," she tells Humaid during a break, opting at that moment not to renew her contract.

"Going? You're not feeling well, *habibe?*"

"No, I mean home. The States." The *States*. She sounds like an asshole. "Time for a change." Bar talk. It's nothing. Like popcorn for dinner.

"You'll come back," says Humaid. "You will see. They say the ex-pat life gets in the blood."

Who says?

Mary Anne is more encouraging. "Good for you! Don't get stuck here. I used to think about leaving, but—I don't know, there's just no reason anymore. I wait for Tahir's checks every month and, *inshallah*, I stay." She sips her piña colada. The sadness around her mouth seems fixed.

"Play 'Candle in the Wind' for me," Mary Anne says. Her crooked earrings flash in the candlelight. "I'm in the mood for a good cry."

•   •   •   •

When Allie's contract is through, Humaid pulls some strings and

Amphibians

books a first class seat for her, Emirates Air, direct to Boston.

"It's the least I can do," he says.

Allie takes the ticket, almost grabs it. They hardly know each other, though they've shared 96 bowls of salted peanuts.

Mary Anne promises to write but doesn't ask for Allie's address.

Allie decides she'll try teaching in Boston. She'll start a new band. She'll play originals, never covers. She'll have to write those originals first.

She'll go to Maine to visit, and one weekend she'll see Scott. Not for nostalgic sex or to boast about her travels—although she wouldn't rule out the pleasure of either— but to buy him a drink and to ask him: What did she look like then? A genuine protégé? Or just a girl who'd kiss him if he told her so?

Both answers would be hard to hear.

•   •   •   •

Emirates Air has a VIP lounge with a bar where Allie sits after checking her bags. What the hell? One farewell Emirati gin and tonic.

In the corner a pianist plays. She bows her head and arches her hands, as though classically trained.

The pianist looks up. It's Maha, the Arab belly dancer, not in veils or sequins, but in a cream trouser suit. Allie can see she's not faking it, not exactly, but she's working hard to remember the notes.

Allie's tempted to ask, booze in her veins, *What about the posh gig in your own club?* Instead she pats her hands together. She's the only one who does.

Maha turns toward her, her eyes no longer kohl-lined. In recognition of her audience, she offers the tiniest of nods.

Ting

Sam lowers herself into the water taxi, now crammed with pale tourists. "You're the dancer," says a large woman in a tie-dyed blouse. "The cancan. Legs!" The woman extends her own leg, pats her thigh. She moves her straw bag to make room.

Sam offers her sober face. She doesn't have to speak to passengers today. She positions her sunglasses and wills the woman to be silent.

"Three dollars," says the boat-guy, the skipper, when exactly twenty passengers have been packed in. He collects the bills neatly, rubbing out creases, lining up heads and tails. He makes change without looking at faces, but when Sam gives him money his lips twitch, as if he's about to laugh or holler. He pushes the wad deep into the pocket of his cut-offs and lets the motor roar, just as a man in a gleaming MS *Sunbeam* cap springs to the edge of the landing.

"Too many," says the skipper, squinting in the direction of the hat. "Next trip." He hops to the stern, busying his hands with rope, straining the muscles in his forearms. His feet are bare and his legs are solidly lean. *Never board a water taxi unless the skipper wears blue*, says the *Sunbeam* leaflet.

Amphibians

The skipper steers out of the harbor slowly, calling out to the other boats and waving with his whole arm. The sun dazzles everywhere until they pass into the shadow of the ship's bow, anchored and white. Five Filipino men in orange coveralls blast a hose along the starboard side, washing away invisible sea-grime. Sam counts down the rows of portholes—A deck, B deck, C deck—but they pass by before she can find her cabin.

Beyond the harbor, the skipper picks up speed and the lady hugs her straw bag to her chest. "We've got a speedy one today," she says. The spray makes little dots on her blouse.

Sam likes this part best, motor wheezing, the race to get there, the sea making things sticky. She sees old wooden houses with porches in faded, pastel paint, high in the hills. Haunted, like Maine houses, the abandoned summer cottages Sam peered inside as a teenager, come fall. There's an old stone fort on the island peak, built by the French? She should walk up there sometime. The passengers never did. Steep road. *Comfortable walking shoes are essential.*

At Grand Anse, the skipper maneuvers around the other water taxis and drops his anchor a few yards from the beach. Sam hops from the bow barefoot, trying to ignore the woman, who follows suit and dangles her leather sandals in her free hand. The woman forms a wary 'o' with her glossed lips because the skipper has reached for her straw bag.

"He'll help you," Sam says.

"Good!" says the woman. "Thank you." And Sam walks on through the shallow waves.

The beach is soon hot on Sam's feet, almost burning, and she likes the feeling. A little girl appears at her side. "Hair bead?" The girl is topless and almost too old to be. She's touching Sam's blonde strands with small fingers, reaching up. Sam shakes her head, removes herself from the girl. She dodges the boys scooting after her and past her, running the length of the beach. "*Waterski-twentydollar.*" A woman under a palm tree nods to Sam, her hands weaving fast, the rest of her body limp and heavy with heat. She makes hats from palm fronds, the wispy leaves dangling out like spokes around the brim. Tonight the passengers will wear them to the Tropical Party on the pool deck and then throw them over the side.

Sam stops before the cooler of ice and bottles and the man crouched over it, his forehead shiny. The glass bottles are green with yellow labels. They've been opened, altered, capped again. "Very strong today," says the man. Sam nods—she's had them before. She takes two and asks for a straw, which the man retrieves from his back pocket, unwrapped. The labels say 'Ting!' and Sam appreciates the name. She'll peel the labels from the bottles when they're empty.

She passes the t-shirt vendors and the ice-cream stand. She'll buy a cone on the way back, maybe nutmeg flavor, the kind Ronnie had last time, a deeper yellow than vanilla with tiny flecks of brown—better than strawberry, or so it looked. He didn't want her germs, not like that. He could be prissy about some things.

At the spice stall, Sam pauses to touch a small straw box with GRENADA spelled out on the lid in red seeds. The R is a little too big, the E a little too small, with little stapled pouches of saffron, cinnamon and cloves inside. She bought one for her grandmother last year and the saffron spice bag opened in her suitcase, leaving yellow dust on her hairbrush, her bra. She can't stop buying them—spiced tea, spiced cookies, a necklace strung with whole nutmegs wound tight with red mace. This she hung above her bunk, next to the picture of her parents, their early days together in Maine.

"Smells like eggnog," said her cabin mate, Pru, from the bottom bunk. Pru had gotten there first.

Sam likes that the spices are strong-smelling, hard to wash

Amphibians

out. She knows just what she'll find in each stall. She's not bored yet, not of Grenada every other Tuesday and not of the ship. She senses she should be bored, but it's an implanted thought—distant, niggling.

At the schoolhouse, Sam stops. The Ting is sweet and fizzy and nearly gone. The buzz is warm and distracting, as planned. The bubbles seem to spread around her chest and explode.

Sometimes, during recess, the schoolhouse is surrounded by kids in red and white uniforms. The boys play cricket in the sand and the girls chase each other to the shoreline, daring each other to wet their little black shoes. But today it's empty, except for a few clucking chickens and a grey goat tied to a tree. A faded cardboard cutout of Santa Claus has been nailed to the schoolhouse door.

On the ship there are Christmas trees in all the lounges. The Sunbeam Band is rehearsing a medley of carols and Pru is bitching about the keyboard parts. On Christmas Day the dancers will wear Santa hats for the cancan number instead of feather headbands. Sam can see herself already: She'll show her teeth. She'll kick as high as she can.

She remembers wrapping red and green yarn around wire hangers, circling and knotting until the dull wire was covered with soft colors. A set of three for her mother with tiny bows beneath the hooks. For her father she gathered loose cloves from the spice drawer and plunged the pointy ends into an orange. It was meant for the truck but he kept it in his sock drawer. Her mother threw it out in February, when the orange was gnarled and brown like a little fist.

"Must be nice," her father's voice said. She'd called him from the pier in Tobago, the pay phone smelling like ketchup. "Get to boss around the other girls."

"And boys. Boy dancers too. It's called being Dance Captain."

"And a boyfriend?" Her Dad winked when he said this, Sam

112

knew. "Handsome fellow, like your father?"

He doesn't know the boyfriend is married.

But Pru knows.

"They're separated," Sam had said, when Pru brought this up.

"What, by water?"

And then Pru didn't say anything else about it.

In public Sam has to call him Captain, just like everyone else. They have to be careful. Sometimes they manage to come to Grand Anse together, but not today.

"I can't un-invite her," Ronnie had said, before the wife arrived.

"I thought you said she wasn't invited." Sam had stayed tucked under the covers and scanned the suite for clues. Ronnie wore a towel around his waist as he shaved, the bathroom door open, his back muscular and tan. He looked serious, older than usual. Sam watched his back for a ripple of something. His eyes in the mirror were very blue.

"If this was twenty years ago." He paused to swish his razor in the foamy little pool he'd made.

"I'd be in Kindergarten," she said.

He didn't smile or scoff but she'd seen it in the angle of his neck, something other than words wrapped up. She saw the trouble she could cause, the inconvenience she'd already become.

She'd wanted the wife to be overweight, a bad dresser. But at the Captain's Ball, right next to Captain Ronnie, the wife was tall and thin with dark hair cut in a slick bob. She nursed champagne with neat sips. She smiled a lot.

Sam drinks the Ting. She spots a money belt and a crumpled blue tee on the schoolhouse porch.

"Hey," a voice calls out from the water. It's the skipper, waist-high in the sea, his chest shining. He looks first at his money belt and then at her.

"Hey," says Sam. She drops her backpack on the sand and twists the cap from the second bottle. The green glass is wet and still a little cool.

"You're drinking the Ting," he says, coming closer, making splashing sounds with his arms.

"Yeah," Sam says. Her voice is far away. She picks at the corner of the label with her thumbnail, careful not to tear it to pieces. She's careful not to look too long at his narrow, sloping waist.

"Peaceful here," he says.

"Nice and quiet."

"And the water is good. Coming in?"

I don't know how to swim. But she can't tell him this—beyond Maine, only Pru and Ronnie know. She looks at her backpack, where her life ring is stored, deflated.

"The water is *good*." He bobs up and down, the waves at his stomach. He's on the verge of laughing at her. "I'm on my break, you know. No worries about me."

She peels the loose corner further, the entire T of Ting. The sun and the bubbles have made everything flustered but it's ridiculously clear to her what will happen.

"You like my boat? Pretty?"

The boat or me? "Sure," she says, so it can be either.

He smiles at this. "You scared of me? The water taxi man?" He's squinting, his eyes unreadable.

She is, a little. She's scared of herself. There isn't an exact moment when she decides. She just stands and pulls off her tank top, then her shorts. She sways a little in her bikini but she feels tall, poised—like a dancer should feel. She wades out to him, her skin cooling. Her teeth ache.

He holds out his arms like he's waiting for a child to fall from a swing. "Come here," he says, which isn't quite right because she's there already. She thinks of Ronnie briefly—the fine blond hairs on his forearms—and then she steps in.

"I can't swim," she tells him.

"No worries," he says, kneeling down until the water reaches his chest. His hands are there at her waist but they're still. "You alone today? Sweet girl like you?"

"I'm not married," she says, "if that's what you mean."

He stops smiling, finally.

"You'll have to be my lifeguard," she says, to make it lighter.

And then his hands move, just slightly, a tiny brush of fingertips against her waist underwater—she feels the familiar pull of something unwise, and then she's kneeling down, knees on ocean bottom; she's leaning in, smelling sweat—*this is a scene in a very bad rom-com*—she's touching her lips to his neck, tasting salt, and then he's kissing her back.

"You'll take my taxi back, right?" He smiles, scooping her up under the knees and lifting her out of the sea and toward the porch of the old schoolhouse. And then it's too late to stop it. She's off the ground, out of the water, away from things that can hold her. A chicken clucks, the goat stares. A few long strides in his arms along the sand and then the boards are hard beneath Sam's back. He slips a condom from his money belt before she even asks, tearing the wrapper with his teeth, but the rest is slow. Little pieces of chipped white paint stick to her skin. She wants to stay on the porch for a very long time. *It's almost Christmas*, she thinks, and lifts her hips to his. She wants him to finish quickly. She touches the back of his neck without thinking and then feels a stab of guilty awareness, sharp but muffled, like a limb falling asleep and tingling itself back to life.

He sighs, resting his brow on her shoulder, breathing hard.

She thinks of the sign she made with a hammer and a piece

of pine scrap from the shop. Everyone else had done NOEL, but in her room, after school, she'd turned on her radio and tapped out holes each night until the hundreds of pockmarks became words: HAPPY HOLIDAYS! Just enough room. There was a knot between the two P's and the DAY was squished. Her father put it on the mantle of the woodstove. That was the year her mother had left for Key West without them.

"I had to act so surprised on Christmas morning," her father had said, years later. "You tapped up there every night like an elf."

She still can't explain the disappointment she'd felt. He'd known. He'd pretended.

On the schoolhouse porch Sam stares at the Santa cutout as the skipper pulls on his shirt. He asks her name and she tells him it's Pru. He says, "You don't want to know mine?" She doesn't, but he tells her anyway: Clarence. He says he'd like to see her again, maybe next time the ship comes in? (He flicks a paint sliver from her knee.) He can meet her on this very porch, if she wants. "I can just be around, you know." He's laughing but there's a trace of loyalty there already, a sense behind the eyes not of duty, but a willingness to continue, if permitted.

She could invent a similar sense of obligation. She could say his name, try it on.

She takes his hand from her knee and drops it, gently. "I don't think so," she says and the rest is simple. He flinches a little and goes.

She'll peel the rest of the Ting label and tape it to a letter or an envelope, maybe a Christmas card.

On Christmas Day, Ronnie will give her a necklace strung with tourmaline. He'll take her out for lobster in Barbados. He'll say something witty about reindeer while holding her hand and swirling his Brandy Alexander.

Sam will touch the sharp stones at her throat and then she'll touch Ronnie's thigh under the tablecloth, politely at first. *Clarence*, she'll think, and then she'll keep touching him. Her cheeks will ache from smiling, a pleasing ache.

Spoils

The old office clock is a fake. Just a glass box outlined in gilt paint—not antique. Gaby imagines the tremor of the painter's hand, how the brush edge shifted, however long ago. The pendulum stops at random times. She watches her father unlatch the little window, bump the hands to the correct Roman numerals and give the ticker a nudge. The sound is like a mug being set down too hard on a table, a confrontation about to begin, over and over. Gaby has to hide to get away.

The photocopier is off limits ever since she was caught with her face crammed in. So, behind the curtain, she crouches and unfolds paper clips, curving them into C-shapes to slide into her mouth as braces. It occurs to her: *I'm stealing from my parents*. Metallic taste. The flat edge of the wire digging into her gums.

This was the bathroom once. Now the room angles back under stairs, covered by an ornate cloth, a magician's cloak of gold and purple. (A fancy bathrobe until her mother plucked the seams and cut the sleeves). On the loose shelf above there are bottles Gaby knows by touch, Windex and Murphy's Oil, a value pack of paper towels, stacks of Post-its and paper clip cartons. There's a medicine cabinet painted shut. (She imagines dead flies and glass vials with rubber stoppers. Poison and truth serum.) There is a useless sink with a ring of crusty green.

She watches the rim of light under the curtain, enough to see passing feet and the base of the brass doorstop: somber Abe Lincoln in a straight-back chair.

At any moment someone might pull back the cloth and find her. But they don't. This is a workspace and the schoolday is done. It's her job to wait until they can get in the too-loud Subaru and go home, just in time for *Grizzly Adams*.

·　　·　　·　　·

Gaby's in the closet when the fisherman arrives. He doesn't close the door. The cold slips under the curtain. The clock has stopped again.

"Can I help you?" says her mother, the receptionist. Her voice is exact, like an auctioneer.

But the fisherman doesn't answer, doesn't pause. Gaby watches muddy rubber boots push along the carpeted hallway to her father's office.

Her mother snaps back the drape. "Go to Grammy's."

But Gaby doesn't move. She studies her mother's knee-high boots and her skirt that is gray felt. A scarf with large maroon circles, interlocking.

"Now."

Gaby leaves her braces in. She thinks to grab Abe Lincoln and a yellow candy from the jar by the clock. She does neither and her mother follows her out.

Between the office and her grandparents' house is another tiny space, the working bathroom. Two doors to remember to latch or someone might burst in and see you squatting. She lifts the latches, closes both doors behind, hears her mother lock the second. She faces the parlor with the dusty piano. The

Amphibians

heaviness of the room makes her tired: her grandfather's collections of opera records and books with frayed, boring spines. The ancient dollhouse with real stainless steel skillets, quarter-sized, which haven't been fun to touch in years.

She sucks on the metal in her mouth and wills herself to drool.

Her grandparents are in the kitchen, as they are every day, slumped against the yellowed Formica table. Her grandfather has his teeth out beside him in a china teacup. He has no need to leave the house but wears a tie. He smells like something sour and wilted. When he wants to, her grandfather can whistle Puccini with impressive vibrato. He can recount details no one else knows or cares about, like James Joyce quotes and Latin phrases.

Today her grandfather isn't whistling. He looks up from his book and stares. He looks like Gomer Pile.

"Hello, there," says Grammy. She wears an apron, felt daisies stitched around the rim. Her long, silver hair is in a bun and Gaby would like to pull it loose and run her fingers through. She brings Gaby a sugar cookie and offers the hardest chair.

Gaby tries not to look into the teacup at her grandfather's teeth. She pulls out her braces and puts them in her pocket. She gnaws on the cookie. She doesn't know what to tell them. She's never come through the second door alone.

"There's a man in the office," she says.

Her grandfather looks out through the window to see the pickup truck with tangled lobster traps.

"One of the Lochman brothers." He lisps without the hardness in his mouth.

"His boots are dirty," says Gaby. "Mom is wicked mad."

"Ha," said Grammy. She has a cackle that's high and funny. She grew up on a farm. She calls Gaby's father *Pickle*. Why she decided to marry the opera-singing judge is a great mystery.

Spoils

Grammy brings more sweets from old boxes—peanut brittle and hard caramels—forbidden at home, and doesn't say, *Watch your teeth*. She peels a potato, using the knife the wrong way, blade toward her rutted fingers. She's never hugged Gaby, but she did give her costume jewelry once, a fat white orchid pin with rhinestones along the ridge and matching earrings, clip-ons, which Gaby wore until her earlobes throbbed.

"He was limping," says Gaby.

"Some crazy fisherman, is all," says Grammy.

"It's the injured fellow," says Grampa.

"Oh," says Grammy. She stops peeling. "Crazy as a shit-house rat."

"Lizzie," says Grampa. "That's the boy with the aneurism."

"What?" says Gaby.

"Accident," Grammy says. "Diving for sea urchins. Your father helped him. That settlement. Had to get him out of jail once."

Gaby sees the mask and the oxygen tank, the urchins on the ocean floor, shaped like Grammy's pincushion. *Spindly little treats for the Japanese*, as her grandfather says. The man had to drop his booty and get back to the surface fast. The creatures got to live, falling quietly to the bottom.

"Assault," says Grampa.

"Shush," says Grammy. "That was some time ago now."

A man who almost drowned, right next door. Gaby feels her own lungs close in. She watches her grandmother chop carrots, then beets. Purple stain on the cutting board. She wishes for more noise—anything—her grandfather's opera records, Latin conjugations. But she can't bring herself to ask him.

So it's quiet, except for the sound of the knife slipping through. The chunks landing in a blue ceramic bowl.

•   •   •   •

Lochman lurches as though drunk, but Daniel, his attorney,

remembers the injury well, the man's leg tangled, his oxygen low. Sea urchins. Good money when lobsters were scarce. Lochman wears a long black coat—flapping, a size too big—and boots pasty with dried mud. He leaves flecks on the carpet Judy vacuumed earlier.

"Lawrence!" he tries. "I wish you'd called ahead." Behind the Congressional flag, loose on its six-foot pole, is a safe, un-locked, and in the safe is a pistol, unused since Daniel's Border Patrol days.

The man's mouth droops, one side slack. "Cheated me," he says. "My mother," he says. "Her money."

"Let's sit down," says Daniel. "Let's talk this through. There was a will, remember? Your mother left a will. But there was no money. I'm sorry. That's how it is sometimes. I'm sorry for—your loss."

Daniel thinks to define it, *pro bono publico*, for the public good. "From the Latin," he begins, but the man reaches into a coat flap, a jerky motion, his eyes dark, his posture unsteady. He smells of kerosene and bait and mildew.

I'm going to die, thinks Daniel. *Shot here in my office in front of the goddamned flag with my daughter in the closet.* He sweeps the flag aside and ducks toward the safe.

But Lawrence holds papers, creased and stained. His moth-er's will, all eight pages. "Nothing left?"

Daniel tries to exhale but the air in his chest feels locked there. He rises slowly, feels the steel heft of the safe behind his knees.

"Have a seat," he says. "I'll take your coat. Judy?" He yells her name, then remembers the intercom, lets it squeak. "Judy! Some tea for Mr. Lochman, please."

On normal days he'd call her Mrs. ah-Wiggins from *The Carol Burnett Show*. They'd laugh and wonder why in God's name they'd bought the gadget.

Spoils

"Is that all you need right now?" says Judy's voice.

"Yes, that will be all. We're fine in here, just fine."

•   •   •   •

Lochman understands he wears the wrong coat. Belongs to his brother. He'd grabbed it on the way out. Took his brother's truck too.

It's just a matter of listening to the words in there. The words are all stacked up. He has to push them out, one by one.

Behind the lawyer's head is a pole with a limp gold flag, touching the ground. Something from Washington DC. Flags shouldn't touch the ground. He shouldn't have come, should have stayed in the house by the sea with his brother and the mice.

He remembers his mother's smell of rot, the way her mouth was a sour, black thing, the sickness inside her seeping out when she opened it. She'd slept with her mouth wide, death leaking everywhere. He'd tried not to breathe too deeply around her.

Then, finding her cold by the woodpile. One final instinct, he guessed—she was cold, she went to get more wood. Crumpled, like a sheet that had blown from the line. Her mouth still gaping. *Pogey*, he'd thought.

The mice, stuck in the traps now. Who would empty them? Still more to be caught. He didn't like the mice. His mother knew this. His mother called him Stinky, like the trapped mice. Like the beer smell on his brother and the death smell from her mouth. His mother gone and still the smell of rotting in the house.

The lawyer is looking at him. Scared but trying not to be. Lochman needs to speak but his mouth doesn't move quickly enough. There are too many words at once and no way to sift through to the good ones. He rumbles with the effort to keep the sentences lined up.

Amphibians

Think first, his mother had told him, even before the accident. As a boy he'd had dreams about running in slow motion. He'd churned and churned but the muscles wouldn't move, like he was stuck in water when it was only air. And then it had actually happened. Stuck in water. The twirl of the rope. The sliced feeling in his lungs. The boy helping him, Brady, who'd died that day. Not a boy, but young. Too young. The pills that made Lochman twitch now.

He saw the looks from children. "Zombie!" said the boy in Hannaford's the other day.

Lochman's red basket, heavy with cans of pea soup, ten for $10.

"Day of the Dead!"

The boy's mother had laughed, then stopped when she saw Lochman's face.

He knew her from high school but couldn't remember her name. She'd played softball, had hickeys on her throat. Worked at the bank now.

"Shush," she said to the boy. "That's not nice."

The lawyer is supposed to fix it. The lawyer is the favorite. Town hero. Golden boy with a fresh, young wife. Mural of his face on the high school wall. Ma said, *The lawyer will help you when I'm gone. Remember? He went to Washington DC and then he came back. When you came up from the dive he helped you. He'll do it again.*

But something hadn't worked. The lawyer hadn't fixed it. There was no money this time.

"Look, Lawrence," the lawyer says in front of the flagpole. "I'm not going to charge you here."

Charge, thinks Lochman. *Electricity. Jousting. Ancient wars.*

"But I can't do much more. We could talk about assets, the house—"

"You can't have the goddamn house!"

"No one's taking your house. The land, I mean—the house. It's worth money if you want to sell. Waterfront property. Out-of-towners willing to pay."

"My mother's house."

"It's your house now, yours and your brother's."

"It's a mouse house."

"Pardon?"

"I need to kill the mice. No one else is going to do it."

He watches the lawyer buzz the intercom again. "Judy," he says. "How's that tea coming?"

•   •   •   •

Judy, locked in the bathroom, is prepared to leap one way or the other. Protect her husband or hide with her child. But she comes out to answer the intercom again, her hands in fists. She clicks the kettle *ON*, rips open Sleepytime, tosses the wrapper in the bin and misses. She thinks to drop a Valium in the crazy man's mug.

Why did they leave DC? Her idea. Romantic. Come back to Daniel's childhood home. Start a family. She remembers the little porch they had in the city. Evenings watching the sun leak away. Wine and her bare skin and Dan's loose fingers on her thigh. Little lights all around them, a comforting swarm of people and houses. She sang in a chorus. They rode horses and drove with the top down. *Congressman's wife*. It was enough then. Why did they change it?

Law school, she thinks again. *Could I hack it? Would I want to?*

Behind her, a thud, a misplaced foot—Abe Lincoln kicked over. Here's the lobsterman, looming, his face a crooked mask, his boots making everything dirty. He lurches out of the office without even looking at Judy or taking his tea. He tries to slam the door behind but it doesn't slam, it bounces back, the door-jamb swollen.

125

Amphibians

"It's all right," says Daniel. His armpits are cups of sweat. "He's just confused. Poor man. His mother meant the world to him."

Judy feels her throat close. *Poor man?*

For months she'll imagine Lochman's truck pulling up their long driveway in the woods. She'll rush to bolt the door when the UPS van comes, thinking it must be him. She'll hold her breath, her heart quick. But it's only her new placemats from Sears, the bulk order of vitamins for Gaby, the new Stetson for her husband for Christmas.

Daniel touches her shoulder.

He takes two butterscotch candies from the ledge below the clock and offers one. She takes it. He nudges the ticker and bumps the hands, his fingers steady. "What a way to make a living," he says, laughing. "I thought he had a gun."

But Judy can't laugh about it yet. The candy is sweet and salty on her tongue. She cracks it in half with her molars.

She goes to get Gaby, who's holding a knife the wrong way with her grandmother in the kitchen. The same worn Formica table, decades old.

"Where's Pickle?" says Gaby, looking up from the potatoes.

Grammy laughs.

Judy tries to smile for them. She tries to make the lock loosen in her ribcage. *How lucky we are. We really are lucky.* It will become an anecdote, the scary man in the long black coat. Dan thought he had a gun, but he was only reaching for the will.

"Why do you call him that? Pickle?" says Gaby to Grammy. But no one in the room can remember.

Freizeit

There are *onsens* in the wilds of Northern Japan, or so they've been told. Hot, earthy cracks in the ground for soaking. Ruthie imagines Old Faithful but cooler, something outdoorsy and borderline catastrophic. Ben disagrees. They're quiet holes, brackish. Tidal pools for humans.

They've been forced to imagine—after two months in Hokkaido, the only *onsens* they've seen are the fake kind, the chlorinated pools in crowded health clubs with fifty-dollar user fees. At Health Barn, which boasts three levels of Jacuzzis, Ruthie peered into the locker room to see a line of Japanese women waiting with towels the size of washcloths.

They left quickly and spent the fifty bucks getting quietly drunk on Sapporo beer in the adjoining bar.

"Lordy, the prices," Ben said, paying the bill. But it was worth it. They were smiling like loons.

•　　　•　　　•　　　•

Ruthie and Ben live in a fancy hotel, brand new, nestled in a vast mall complex. From their corner suite they can see Otaru Harbor. Little boats sweep by and big ferries slide into the jaws of the terminal. They're closer to Russia than to Tokyo and so there are people who look like them everywhere, women with sharp cheekbones and pale skin, and large men with chest hair. Ruthie is somewhat Russian, she remembers, on the Kaplan side. While pacing the floors of the mall, she sometimes pretends to be non-American. There are rumors about places like Health Barn. No Russians allowed.

When not in the mall, Ruthie perches on the hotel mezzanine with her laptop in a corner chair facing the sea. No one bothers her there, and so she reads old emails and attempts to create haikus. (The first and last lines come quickly—the middles are hard.) The laptop gets hot and feels heavy on her thighs, and the screen seems to be bombarding her with unhealthy particles. Her head aches when she's done, but there's a dull pleasure in it too.

One night in the hotel bar she tells Ben she wants to go back to school to study more. She isn't sure what, just more. He nods when she said this, then clinks his glass with hers.

• • • •

Ben is the hotel's visiting Food and Beverage Manager, which is why, at the General Manager's monthly cocktail reception, he winks at Ruthie and says, "I manage the bevvies *quite* well." He was a chef once; he was Head Chef when Ruthie met him aboard the MS *Sunbeam*. He had a suite on the bridge, right next to the Captain's quarters, and because Ruthie was the Fitness Captain, she felt she deserved to live there too. They ate oysters and finished the leftover bottles from passenger tables, the expensive dregs of reds and whites.

Now Ben is a traveling Food and Beverage doctor. He hires, taste-tests and markets in Asia, the Middle East, Northern Africa. He's in and out in six months, a year tops, leaving the crew intact (head chef, sous chef, pastry chef, sommelier), leaving

Freizeit

a local chef with his title, a hotel policy. Most F and B guys prefer the longer jobs in Dubai or Bangkok or Majorca, Ben had explained to his father, back in Newcastle. They got used to their cars and corner suites, their weathered beach loungers, their local girlfriends. Too much flying made them weary and constipated.

But it suits you, Benji, his father had chimed in at the pub. *You're young.* And single, he meant, although Ruthie had been sitting right there.

When asked, Ruthie sometimes lies and says they're married. In Abu Dhabi she bought rings, two thin bands she found in the Gold Market, because it was illegal to share a hotel suite out of wedlock. She wears hers still, sometimes on the left hand, sometimes on the right.

Ruthie has a vague belief that someday they'll have several rooms of their own, not in a hotel. She wants at least one room she doesn't have to share with Ben, quiet and smoke-free, with her CDs alphabetized. She wants a place to store her photo albums in a pretty town where the currency is familiar and wine bars are near. She will not be required to wear makeup and heels to dinner and she'll have one or two close female friends to bitch to in a healthy way.

It's August and they have four more months to go, with the possibility of a Singapore job after Christmas.

And so, after work each night, Ben strips down to his Calvin Klein's and wears his headphones with the super-long wire. He watches *Charlie's Angels* reruns as Ruthie reads *Runner's World*, sent from home. This is their latest compromise, like the air-conditioning on half-blast and smoking allowed only in the hallway.

Mornings, Ruthie's jaws ache. She has to massage her cheeks for a moment or two. She runs her tongue over her rigid molars and imagines they've become smooth as polished stone.

Amphibians

At the next cocktail party, Ben finds Ruthie on the outskirts and whispers, "Come say hello." Then he steers her into the thick of it.

"Ruthie makes haiku," says Ben.

She braces herself, sensing that her bra strap is showing and that the crisp, jeweled wife of the GM is eyeing it.

Ben laughs a little, kindly, to fill the gap, and the GM's wife laughs too.

•   •   •   •

They buy a motorcycle, or Ben buys a motorcycle and Ruthie feels she should contribute. They spend several days in second-hand bike shops writing down questions about mileage and cylinder size and insurance. They receive written responses from the Japanese sales staff in near-perfect English. (No one wants to risk incorrect grammar out loud, Ruthie and Ben included.) Ben chooses a green bike, with Honda TRANS-Alp lettering on the side and a seat large enough to accommodate two. (Ruthie asks him test it with her it in the store, to make sure she won't slide off.) They buy helmets, a bike lock, a waterproof bike cover, saddlebags for storage, wind and water-resistant pants and jackets and gloves. Ruthie chooses purple and Ben chooses racing green, to match the bike. They go to CAMPLAND and buy small, lightweight versions of things: a gas stove, two collapsible stools, a tent that fits inside a sock.

"Like Star Wars figures. Matchbox cars," Ruthie says, carrying the tent to checkout. Things she'd once collected, she means. Easy to pack up and carry somewhere else.

•   •   •   •

On Ben's day off, they try again to find an *onsen*, an outdoor one. Ruthie studies the piece of map flattened against her thigh, searching for some sign of it on the page. Three times they've circled the campground path, just wide enough for the bike, and three times the same nervous campground attendant had frowned at the engine, the noise.

"Stop it! Turn it off!" Ruthie says, yelling into Ben's back.

They park; they peel off their helmets, their layers of windbreaker. Ben lights a cigarette and says, "We need tuition."

He's British, he speaks this way, and so Ruthie has learned to interpret. This one is new. He's busying himself with the saddlebags and the cooler, the interlocking bungee cords that keep everything in place.

He means, *We need help. We have no idea what we're doing.*

By the time she understands, Ben has gathered some kindling for their fire and washed his hands with a mini bar of hotel soap in lake water. He's enlisted the graying campground attendant, who leads them down a steep path, toward a row of metallic shacks. Inside one they find a small wooden tub, cauldron-like, barely enough room for two—something Ma Ingalls would fill with kettle water from a stove. The lower half of the tub is lined with steel, and underneath the tub there's a hole, a space to build a fire. The attendant gestures with his arms: *You fill the tub with icy water from the hose. You chop the wood. You stack the wood. You light the match. You cover the tub, like a boiling pot. You wait for the boil to cool; you get in.*

Ruthie and Ben nod. He leaves them to it.

It's getting dark and four Japanese teenagers emerge from the adjacent tub shacks, damp and flushed. To Ruthie they don't look as though they've been naked together in hot water, drinking beer. They're folding their towels into tiny squares and sealing them in plastic bags. They're placing their bottles in the recycling bin. They mime in Ruthie's direction, offering to chop wood, and she refuses, miming back.

"It's getting dark," Ruthie says, and Ben agrees.

"So that's an *onsen*," he says.

Amphibians

"I don't think so. It's supposed to be natural. In the ground. This is just an old-fashioned hot tub."

They cook instead, hands busy, in a roofed communal cooking area with little cement benches and square pits with grills. The sun had set and so they cut and slice by poorly aimed flashlight, reluctant coals. Ruthie arranges the pre-sliced veggies on a towel, leaning in an awkward way, and Ben saws through the meat with his Swiss Army Knife. They assemble the kebab cubes of beef with green peppers and mushrooms squeezed in between. Ben stokes their little pit. Ruthie preps the baked potatoes and readies the condiments: butter squares swiped from the hotel café, packets of barbecue sauce and salt stored in a contact lens container.

They drink, first the mini bottles of Chardonnay from the cooler, then the little bottles of scotch mixed with warm Coke. When this runs out, they try the beer in the vending machine, Sapporo, the preferred brand in Hokkaido, it seems. It's five dollars a can but they drink anyway. Beer in vending machines! They take turns. He buys two, she buys two, walking the long stretch to the glowing machine, plunking in the one hundred-yen coins. The fire wriggles before them and they can't seem to look away from it; the more they drink, the more insistently it burns. They talk quietly about the veggies and the meat and the stars and the motorcycle and the smells in the air and what they'd do tomorrow. Hike? Swim? Sleeping in is never an option, although Ruthie wants it to be. They don't mention the empty hot tub shack.

They're closer there, Ruthie believes, away from the hotel life they've chosen. They can drink more and not be caught by Managers.

When they don't talk, they read. Ben takes possession of the pocket-sized *Lonely Planet* phrasebook, practicing verb tenses he'll never use. Ruthie squints at the front page of *The Japan*

Freizeit

Times, absorbing only random details: Usu, where the volcano is cooling down, Yokosuka, where the USS *Kitty Hawk* has docked.

They clean up, wobbly as they stand. The cooking area has one stainless steel sink large enough for a human body, with freezing water running through the single faucet. Ruthie washes the dishes quickly, six concentric pans with lids that doubled as plates, like the rainbow colored beach buckets she'd had, the largest red cupping the smallest purple and the rest in between. She could mention this to Ben—*my beach buckets*—but it seems too complicated to explain.

In the bathroom, with one fluorescent light bulb and moths flapping desperately, Ruthie brushes and flosses and moisturizes. Ben pees against a tree stump. She hears the swooshing from inside. And then she's standing outside the tent with him, clutching her plastic toiletry bag. She's waiting for Ben to switch on the flashlight, which he does, and together they dive in, zipping up the flap quickly behind them, scanning the tent walls for beasties, which is Ben's word for bugs. Ruthie turns to him. She's high enough to go for it. She kisses Ben hard and his breath is tar and oil and she's minty and his lips are so small but she keeps going, she's clawing and humping like a crazed raccoon. *Stay awake!* she orders. But his limbs are dead heavy, as though he's spent the day lifting boulders.

She stops. *Too drunk to onsen,* she thinks and it seems almost funny, and this is her last coherent thought before sleep, which is a swift, final thud.

She wakes an hour later with a dry mouth and a sinking panic. (*Is it just the booze or has something else happened?*) It's quiet. Ben's arm is heavy on her stomach, pressing into her bladder. She has to pee. She pushes at the arm. (He stirs, turns away.) She has to *go*, so she unzips, stumbles out, trips in a shallow ditch, feels a sharp and exhilarating twinge in her ankle that wakes her completely. The pain becomes something throbbing and consistent—a relief—and so she stays where she is, crouching, and pees in the ditch. She feels mosquitoes on her back, slaps at them. She pees on her toes and swears and wipes them dry with a flap of Ben's shirt and then she's weeping, great heavy gulps of it pouring out of her. They can hear her probably, the other campers, but she can't make herself stop.

When she's able to breathe again she counts the months. She feels sober then, though she knows she isn't, and the number sinks in and she allows it to. There's a panic-tension in her belly not unlike the having-to-pee feeling. *Seven months.* She slaps at more bugs. Someone stirs in a nearby tent and so she moves. She breathes. She wipes her eyes and unzips the flap again, fast. She crawls back in.

•   •   •   •

Ben had brought it up first, the camping idea. They were on the crew deck on Ruthie's night off, sailing out of Malta for Sardinia. They were drinking leftover wine and holding hands under a ship blanket, side by side on sun loungers, the plastic slats greasy and worn. The sea was black and still and the engine churned below. He said, "I wish we were in a tent right now," and Ruthie thought first of ham and cheese sandwiches.

When Ruthie was seventeen, she and her boyfriend Nelson went camping because it was cheaper than a hotel room and because there were trees around, and the earnest smells of wood smoke and pine needles. Ruthie could say to her parents, upon her return, "It was great. We hiked and got some pictures from the summit. Yeah, it was pretty busy. We played Frisbee." Which they had, briefly, before getting high from a Sprite can bong and retiring to the tent to undress. They ate the ham and cheese sandwiches they'd bought from Shop N'

Save. They drank beer, which Ruthie was still learning to like. They smoked some more from the Sprite can. It was a heavenly kind of privacy, there in the damp, flushed space of their little dome. They could be heard, but they couldn't be touched.

"We should do that, go camping," Ben said. She squeezed his hand by way of answer and they resumed their drinking and sea gazing as Malta became smaller and smaller and then nothing.

They flew to Maine during their next break from the ship, to visit her parents. It was summer and the campgrounds were packed. Ruthie hadn't unfolded her tent in years, but she remembered exactly how to put it up, how to poke the poles through the color-coded slots. She did this quickly and Ben nodded, impressed. He crawled inside the dome to spread out the bedding and Ruthie took a long drink from her water bottle and when Ben emerged, his face was set like rock. He lit a cigarette.

He'd found a triangular corner of a Trojan wrapper in the corner, a tiny scrap of her teenage self.

Ruthie later wondered why they hadn't laughed about it. She felt the option stretching before them for a full second or two, knowing it wasn't going to happen. Instead they bickered quietly until a bearded father appeared near their site to retrieve his daughter's baseball. Ben ran out of cigarettes and then there was nothing left to do but drink themselves senseless and hope for peace in the morning.

But already something fierce had risen up in Ruthie, a self-protective instinct, like her mother throwing her arm across the passenger seat when braking. Already she was hardening her stomach against him, preparing.

In the morning they went swimming in the lake for distraction. Ruthie dried off before him and dozed on her towel, dreaming about the ship, about Rise and Shine Aerobics. (She had to start in five minutes and couldn't find her headset mic.) When she woke, Ben's sneakers were there, beside her. She waited, trying to read her book. The glare of the sun made her a little dizzy and she wanted water or a Slush Puppy. This would make them laugh and forget maybe, blue tongues and ice.

Ben was a solid swimmer, arms slicing through with clean strokes. In Curacao they swam two miles one day, resting on a jagged rock near the shore, kissing and tasting salt and catching their breath and daring each other to swim naked, which they had, with their suits hooked around their necks.

On the lake there were speedboats and she couldn't find his face. She kept scanning heads and bodies in the water and still couldn't see him. She was breathing quickly, she was very hot—she got up, she gathered their things, she unlocked the car and turned the key. She snapped off the radio to think.

She found him three miles away, barefoot in the dirt of the shoulder, jogging in his swimming trunks.

"Cheers," he said, getting in the car. His voice was rigid and so she didn't bother clutching at him, as planned. He wouldn't look at her, but somehow she knew he'd be willing to laugh about this, much later, willing to bury this day and let her live with it. This is how they would have to love each other, by careful diversion, by swallowing.

What if he'd drowned? The creepy possibility of it lasted like a stain. She'd be to blame. She hadn't watched him carefully enough.

On the other hand, if he was dead, she'd likely have sex again.

Terrible, she thought of the thought. But also a little bit funny. She could be funny still.

•   •   •   •

Freizeit

Ruthie drops the *onsen* idea for a while. She goes to the health club on the top floor of the mall, called Freizeit. A solid German-sounding name for Japanese clientele. Membership includes access to the ten-lane swimming pool, the waterslide, the sushi bar, the massage studio, the aerobics studio and the tranquility chamber. There are vending machines stocked with toothbrushes, deodorant, anti-cellulite cream, trail mix, juice boxes, carob treats, beer and cigarettes.

Ruthie likes being the only blond-haired person at Freizeit. No Russians, she's notices. Maybe they really aren't allowed.

She goes to the chamber first, which is like an airplane cabin with reclining chairs in rows. There are stacks of thin green blankets, sweet-smelling in a chemical way. There are Japanese men in bathrobes with blankets draped around their bare legs, or slung over their heads to block out the light, or gripped in their hands for comfort. They sleep or stare at the soundless TV's, which are set to different channels and bolted high on the peach-trimmed wall.

Ruthie fiddles with her trail mix packet. The men stir, confused. She imagines lifting their blankets, stroking them quietly, muffling their groans with a firm hand over their mouths.

She gets up. Time to move. Her classmates greet her warily. (*Ohio-goes-eye-mass.*) But they make room. They let her stand in the very front row. The aerobics instructor checks to see if Ruthie understands and of course she does—she can count to four in Japanese (*itchy, knee, sun, she);* that's all she needs to know. The grapevines and box steps and power squats are universal moves, it seems.

After class, she showers. Everyone else sits on white plastic stools where countless bare asses have been, blasting away at crevasses with shower nozzles. This is their bathing ritual, Ruthie knows: bright lights, clean skin. It should be impossible to think about anything except getting dressed quickly. But she inspects them, these women who've given birth, who've made love to their husbands for decades, probably. Their imperfect bodies that still manage to attract. She watches two old women with tiny towels and loose skin. They dry their sparse, spidery pubic hair with blow dryers, digging free Q-tips into their ears, inspecting the results. They laugh in Ruthie's direction and then to each other. They stop laughing, and share secrets. She's a minor distraction only.

Which imperfections are most offensive? Hers or his?

There are no curtains, and Ruthie is the only one standing to bathe, the only one stooping back and forth to squirt shampoo and conditioner from the blue and green bottles on the tiled floor. *Blue* for sham*poo*. She's overcoming obstacles in a resourceful way, a good little camper.

In the Grooming Center, where there are soft, flattering light bulbs, she feels better. There are bottles of hairspray and red plastic combs stored in a germ-killing machine that looks like a toaster oven. There's a centrifugal spinning device for drying bathing suits in thirty seconds. There are heated toilet seats. And there are children everywhere, plunked on the floor on Freizeit towels—clean, sucking on juice boxes. Ruthie watches them.

Then she dresses, deodorizes, applies eyeliner and lip gloss. She takes her place on the mezzanine and tries again to write haiku.

•   •   •   •

Ruthie and Anne, the Pastry Chef's wife, meet for coffee. They do this weekly and order European things—*café au lait*, croissants. They talk about the hotel or the touristy things they should be doing, or the meanings of the kanji symbols on the menu. Anne is Chinese—she met Klaus during his previous contract in a Beijing hotel—but everyone assumes she's from

Freizeit

Otaru, even some of the locals. The café waitress frowns when Anne orders in English.

After the coffee, they go to the supermarket on the first floor and Anne teaches Ruthie the symbols for chicken and beef, low fat and regular. Ruthie smiles and makes a great show of memorizing, but doesn't.

That night, Ben and Ruthie are invited for drinks in Anne and Klaus' suite, one floor down. Klaus opens a bottle of whiskey and Anne provides plates of cheese and crackers and coleslaw. Ben digs in and Klaus smokes and Anne opens the window.

"Once you know what to do, it's very relaxing," says Klaus. "It's a very relaxing clean." He's talking about the *onsen* they found the weekend before, in a little town just one hour away.

"You wash first," says Anne. "Then you soak. You must wash first, they are very particular."

Klaus rips the page from his map-book and Ruthie has to stop herself from saying, "Don't!" Ben decides they'll find the *onsen* that weekend, for sure, and they all drink to this, although Ruthie has had enough and wants only to go back to their suite and hold her book in her hands.

Klaus tells them, again, that Freizeit meant 'free time' and that he and Anne can't join because they have matching tattoos on their shoulder blades, the kanji symbols for Happiness. Anne says she thinks the no-tattoo-rule has something to do with Triad gangs, but Ruthie thinks it has something to do with superstition and hygiene. Maybe the traces of skin-ink are thought to contaminate the water, she says.

An empty moment follows.

When they take the elevator back to their room Ben says, "*Onsen*, then?" He throws an arm around her shoulder and pretends to choke her, gently. It's a rhetorical question and so she chooses not to answer. In their room, Ben reaches for his headphones.

Amphibians

In her dream, they're in adjacent *onsens*, divided by gender, and Ben loves it. He gets into an elaborate miming act with a naked Japanese man and charms him and Ruthie is left alone, with no one to mime to. *Pathetic,* she tells herself in the dream. *Just make some friends of your own.*

·　　　·　　　·　　　·

In the morning, Ruthie receives an errand. She must buy new sneakers, for both of them. She whines a little—she feels like whining. She says to Ben, "I don't know what you like."

"Get Nike or Adidas. No Japanese knock-offs." He says *awe*-dee-*doss* and she corrects him and he smiles quickly. He's tying his tie in front of the steamed bathroom mirror, peering into a streak of clear space he's made with his palm. This will leave streak marks and she almost tells him so. *She* doesn't have to clean it, so why should she care? That's what he'd say. She grabs her wallet, her keys, her gym bag, pre-packed the night before. She lets the door close behind her firmly.

Most of the rules in Freizeit have to do with shoes. At first Ruthie wore her sneakers past reception, into the locker room. She sailed past the beaming receptionist and no one stopped her, no one so much as glanced footward. Instead the Freizeit manager called the hotel General Manager, who then called Ben into his office to explain: His wife must purchase a pair of shoes for the gym only, never to be worn outside.

What other rules is she breaking without even being aware?

Later, in Freizeit, having bought the most expensive pairs of sneakers in the mall, Ruthie bends to retrieve her special cleansing bar (clear, honey-colored, meant to replenish), a twinge cuts into her spine and makes her stop mid-stoop. She breathes out slowly—the pain is sharp and persistent and lodged in a low vertebra—and she focuses on the concentric circle-holes of the shower drain. She remembers she's exposed, curtain-less.

Freizeit

But it passes, and she straightens. Ben doesn't know about the twinges and won't. She isn't prepared to reveal this yet, her obvious deficiency.

"Your wife," the GM had said. She wonders if Ben had corrected him. She hasn't worn her Abu Dhabi ring in weeks.

●   ●   ●   ●

On Ben's night off they fight again. Ben grabs his wallet from the nightstand.

Off to grab a pint, Ruthie predicts.

But Ben stays fixed in the doorframe and stares at the floor. "Ruthie," he finally says.

It's just a beer, for Christsakes—

But he doesn't say that either. He says, "Let's not do this— this tearing strips from each other." His face is soft. Ruthie imagines the strips of string cheese she used to get in her lunchbox, little satisfying threads to peel and consume.

She tells him this, and he leaves.

When she sees him next it's 3:00 AM and he reeks of Scotch. He's smiling. "*Cheese*, Ruthie? What's fucking wrong with you?"

Ruthie wants to remember how his face had looked before he left, but it's gone, crowded out by what she's done in the four-hour interim (called her Nana with her phone card, listened to Seal, George Michael and Sade, separated their laundry into whites and colors and placed the bags outside the door, read forty-three pages of *Tender Is the Night*, borrowed from Anne, consumed two and a half generous glasses of Japanese Chardonnay ("Good to Free Your Mind and Relaxing Conversation," says the label).

Instead of answering Ben, she closes her eyes and summons the characters: crazy Nicole Warren and dandy Dick Diver and the precocious Rosemary Spears. She gives them outfits and expressions. She and Ben had been like that once, pretty expats abroad. They'd been good in water, on beaches. Entwined and buoyed by the sea.

When sleep finally comes, Ruthie dreams she's reeling off endless knock-knock jokes into a plastic Karaoke microphone. Ben laughs politely from the front row and this is enough—she knows if she can make him laugh she can keep him there.

Late morning, from somewhere in his boozy fog, Ben shifts and suddenly squeezes her hand.

"I *do* love you."

Something in Ruthie's stomach dissolves a little, but her jaw stays locked shut. She can't tell which one of them he's trying to convince. She doesn't say it back.

•   •   •   •

When they finally do hunt for Anne and Klaus' *onsen*, it's mid-October, their last trip of the season, before it gets too cold and too dangerous on the bike, before it begins to snow. Ruthie wears twelve pieces of clothing in all, including two pairs of socks—she counts, from skin up, as they speed along. They have detailed directions and they're fully prepared: extra sweaters, extra towels, fire-starters, charcoal blocks, maps in English and in Japanese, a full tank of gas. It's brittle and fresh and Ruthie is hanging on to Ben's waist, the broadness of him, as they zip over small hills and under boughs of turning leaves. The Hokkaido roads are thick with trees, like Maine.

In the morning, they hike. It's sunny, a freak spell of fall warmth. The trail is longer and steeper than expected, and Ruthie keeps slipping. The leaves underfoot are wet and her old ankle sprain buzzes a little, reminding her, but she ignores it and stays upright.

They're panting from the elevation, from the beer and Scotch the night before, breathing it out into the hills, like dragon's breath. (She'll use this in a haiku, Ruthie thinks—*like dragon's breath*.) She likes this, feeling winded and absorbed, likes the burning in her chest, the idea of imaginary creatures.

"Okay?" Ben turns around to look at her, sweat marking the collar of his shirt.

"Yup," she says. She's thinking: *We have it all wrong—the* onsens *can't possibly exist, just a* Lonely Planet *hoax*.

He's looking at her like he did in the doorway.

At the top they find a bedraggled rope swing hanging from a steep branch, Tarzan style, and Ruthie thinks of the boy who died, falling from the rope swing at West Harbor Pond, how she hadn't really known him and how her father had cried with relief that it hadn't been her. She scratches at a scab on her back, a bug bite scar Ben hasn't seen. She digs in her fingernails, drawing blood, bending her shoulder in an unnatural way to reach.

They finish the hike. They have to pack up quickly to make it back in time, before dark. They'll have to lie to Anne and Klaus and tell them the *onsen* had been fantastic.

Ruthie clings to him, all the way home.

•   •   •   •

In December, in Freizeit, there are giant Telly Tubby-shaped Santas hanging from ceilings and smaller ones sticking to lamps and to the nametags of fitness trainers. At the reception desk there's one with a maniacal laugh, dancing like Elvis from the waist down. This is in bad taste for many reasons, Ruthie thinks, removing her shoes. Won't the children be startled, the wonder of *all those chimneys* diminished by logic? (*All those Santas*.) But in the locker room the children are calm—they've been plopped on the floor and are wrapped in towels. Again the moms wipe and brush and pat them clean and seem not to worry.

Ruthie does a step class, the hi-impact portion accompanied

by a remix of "Flashdance, What a Feeling." The song is still in her head as she does her extra sit-ups and push-ups on her private corner mat. When she's done, Ruthie heads to the tranquility chamber, intent on her reward: a packet of carob-coated raisins. Tucked beneath a sweet-smelling blanket, she allows herself to doze.

That's when she finds it, a brand new sign in Japanese and an arrow. She follows (feeling brave and warm under the soft blanket cloth)—*What a feel-ing!*—down one flight, two, and there they are, two pristine cloth curtains, the black kanji symbols for man and woman. And, through glass, a steaming, secluded pool in actual earth.

She strips down and stashes her sweaty gym clothes in the cubby provided. She rinses the stool first, with hot water. She allows herself to sit. She squirts a palm full of white gooey soap. (Or shampoo? The colors are different.) She lathers, taking her time. There's no twinge in her back or ankle and a mirror reflects it all.

She opens the French doors and steps outside and it's gorgeous there, the air rigid, the steam rising, a fence dividing the men's and women's sides. The pool is shallow and so she squats and slides like an eel along the bottom, which isn't muddy, but hard and smooth, like baked clay. She smells mushrooms and a pleasant kind of algae—salad smells, clean and edible. She stands up, letting the chill seep in just enough—then she squats back down again fast, feeling goosebumps dissolve, wondering if there are boats beyond the fence, moving through the almost-Russian harbor.

She invents a secret crack in the dividing fence and through it she places Ben, all eyes and wet curls. He's lovely to see, and smiling plainly. He makes a face at her and disappears.

Fishing

Underwater, something unexpected and slippery oozes between Sam's toes. Oil?

Valdez, she thinks. *All those shriveled, blackened birds.*

It isn't black, Sam sees, lifting her foot flamingo-style to examine. It's dark brown and gritty and thicker than expected, like taffy or molasses. "Thick as a board," Ronnie sometimes says, usually in reference to a wine steward. He means stupid, slow, and Sam feels that way lately. *Thick*. Like her brain has become sludge.

It's Rome Day, which is why Sam swims in Civitavecchia Harbor. Several hours earlier, during Tours Duty, she'd directed 1053 ship passengers onto twenty tour busses for the "When In Rome" excursion (Coliseum, Pantheon, Forum, Spanish Steps, Trevi Fountain and Saint Peter's).

For Sam, Civitivecchia is the worst stop on the Med itinerary. Hard to pronounce and ugly. ("Industrial," says Ronnie.) The MS *Sunbeam* gleams fluoride-white next to its poor cousin cargo ships—black with algae, drooping at their berths. Port-side there are robotic cranes and boxy old containers and greased men in coveralls. The nearest public beach, where Sam

Amphibians

now wades, is a thirty-minute taxi ride from the gangway, just a small stretch of sand with a unisex bathroom and a phone booth. Not a single *gelato* stand.

Ronnie doesn't mind. He's been fishing all morning at the peak of a low and jagged rock-pile, the blunt handle of his telescopic rod clamped to his hip. In the neat plastic compartments of his tackle box he keeps hooks, lines, lures, sinkers and a Swiss Army Knife with his initials engraved. For bait he uses worms first, then squid, which he begs from the ship's kitchen staff. "Squid tentacles," he explained, curling his fingers into spidery squid claws. "They stay in the hook better. Not the heads."

But Ronnie, now wormless, peels back the Tupperware lid to find heads that are purple, plum-sized, cut open at one end like finger-puppets. He says something about this but Sam ignores him. *Ca*-la-*ma*-re, she thinks, a nice Italian word, a little song. She dips her fingertips into the still, gray sea and wishes they had champagne. If she squints she can make out the *Sunbeam* bow, a tiny white blotch far away.

She remembers in Maine there was a tidal pool, a hermit crab, a class trip to the beach. The hermit crab's body was closed tight like a nut.

"Sing to it," said Mrs. Blake, and Sam did, a hymn her father liked. As she sang the nut opened up, one leg and then another, until the whole thing was living on her hand. She'd tried to stay still but couldn't—she dropped it, a little glad to have it gone from her skin.

"It responds to sound waves," said Mrs. Blake, but Sam didn't believe her. It was her voice in particular. *It responds to me.*

Sam inches her way back to the rock pile, studying Ronnie on its tip. He's trim for his age, no love handles yet, although he worries about it, watches what he eats at the Captain's Table, opts for lobster bisque instead of tenderloin steak. His chest is hairy, a little white, and Sam likes tugging on it before she has to rise for Plunge Pool Paddle. When they're still cocooned, bedridden. Before their duties begin.

She used to have calluses, blisters, real dancer's feet. In Boston, before she got the ship callback, she'd taken class every day, sometimes twice. She'd been a temp, a Kelly girl, and on the days she wasn't filing or stuffing envelopes at Government Center, she auditioned. Her ballet teacher said she should move to New York, that's where she'd find the real work, but Sam couldn't quite make herself leave.

"You can always teach," her mother said. But it sounded like a failure's option.

The MS *Sunbeam* audition was held at the end of the summer, after a series of cruise callbacks. The accompanist crouched at a battered piano, and a bald man sat behind a long table, not yet scowling. The audition studio was smaller than Sam's apartment.

"Pirouette?" the bald man asked, and Sam did a triple without even thinking. After that she was blocked in the center, six nights a week.

•   •   •   •

Ronnie slices squid heads with his knife, making due, pinning bits of creature onto hook and wiping his hands clean with a *Sunbeam* washcloth the color of tangerines. There are procedures he follows. He was a Scout for a long time, much longer than most boys, and to Sam this makes sense. Other kids would have teased him. (*Seventeen and still building fires?*) His sash covered with badges. Sam would have teased him.

"Disgusting," says Sam, so Ronnie will descend to inspect her foot. He does this, leaning in to see. She thinks of pulling his head to her stomach or touching his cheek in sultry way.

But he speaks. "Oil. I warned you." And soon he's back in position on the pile, about to cast.

Amphibians

Sam smells her fingers. Tar. "It feels like molasses."

"Me lass is on the table," says Ronnie, jerking the line. He's not looking at her anymore. "I'd start scrubbing if I were you."

"I need soap."

"Try the loo. Or try the *Russians*." He winks. He winks a lot lately, when he doesn't know what else to say. "They look like they come prepared."

The Russians have just arrived, their sun dresses flapping as they climb from the cab. They're the two cocktail waitresses from the Showboat Lounge—Olena and someone else, someone who doesn't always wear her name badge. Sam waves and Ronnie gives her a familiar look, meaning, *Don't be too obvious about us.*

"Good lord," says Sam. "Everyone knows."

Olena strips down to a yellow bikini and her body is moonish, pocked. She bends over to spread her towel, her back to them, her bikini riding up, and Ronnie, as Sam expects, says, "Holy." What surprises Sam is his next line, whispered: "Just like two enormous . . . *cantaloupes*." He uses his free hand, the clean hand, and cups an imaginary melon slice, about to take a bite. He grins for Sam, winking. "Honeydew?" He bares his teeth, little incisors. She sometimes thinks of vampires, of sucking, but today she thinks of barnacles, dry and crusty, and how they used to shred her feet when she was small.

The fruit reference is supposed to be a private joke—it's supposed to remind Sam of her own rear, and how Ronnie had first squeezed it two years ago in the life-jacket storage closet. "Fruit-like and firm," Ronnie had concluded, and it was such an odd, dirty-old-man thing to say that she'd snorted at him, which had made Ronnie giggle too. Then they undressed each other quickly in the dark.

At first they'd made an effort to be discreet. During the Captain's Ball they stood at opposite ends of the lounge. Sam sneaked to Ronnie's suite only during the Staff Captain's watch. She'd been sharing a cabin with Pru on C-deck and after the first few times, after the non-teeth-brushing phase, she brought a toiletry bag—floss, a tiny comb. Soon she left a day uniform, so she wouldn't have to wear her evening dress back, her mascara smudged, her hair knotted, a short length of passenger area to cross before she reached a Staff Only door—fifteen paces. The cabin stewards saw her. Or the engineers, below deck, appearing from behind heavy doors and releasing fumes of exhaust, a steady roar of machinery. They looked away. Or other dancers—Gayle or Tina—on their way to the crew mess for coffee.

"Good night?" they said.

The walk of shame. A fling. Gayle probably thought it could be her next week.

Ronnie lit candles for her at first, and ordered private meals. He opened champagne. Until Sam's toothbrush wasn't in her toiletry bag but right beside Ronnie's on the fake marble sink.

At the Captain's Ball, he forgot and touched her low on the waist.

Val, the Cruise Director, called Sam in. She tapped a maroon fingernail on a Post-it pad. She said, "Ship Policy" and "Written Warning." Sam told Ronnie, and Ronnie called in Val. Nothing more was said.

For a while, when Sam entered a room, Ronnie looked for one hard moment, even with other Officers around. She was used to stares, but this was different. It felt like laughing gas. She was high and a little nauseous.

• • • •

In the unisex bathroom Sam runs the tap and squirts a palm-full of watery pink soap from the dispenser. It's a nice foot, she thinks, narrow and ballerina-arched. She scrubs first with her hands and then with paper towels from a broken dispenser. The sink turns mealy brown.

Olena appears behind her and says "Katastroph." She frowns down at her own smeared toes. "No good."

"Try some soap," Sam says, scootching out of the way.

Olena smiles and hoists the foot, letting it land evenly on the counter. "Your husband, I think, is a pervert, no? Just a little bit." Her nipples are two dark splotches under her bikini top. "He looks like your father?"

Sam considers this. "Maybe. He's not my husband."

"He is age of your father, I think."

Sam isn't sure what to say. *Haven't you seen us together before?*

They scrub together without talking. Olena makes fast progress, loose black strands framing her cheeks, damp against her pink skin.

Olena isn't there to judge, Sam decides.

She remembers, not long after the storage closet squeezing but before the toothbrush transfer, Ronnie took Sam to a topless beach in Nice, unknown to passengers. Sam left the gangway first, smiling sweetly at Joe on security. She felt like a Charlie's Angel. She wore a wrap-around mini-skirt and a tight halter-top, like all French women seemed to in summer, like Farah Fawcett might. She sipped tepid *café au lait* in a back street coffee shop, legs crossed, sunglasses on, until Ronnie arrived one hour later, as planned. He was out of uniform, in his "civvies"—red shorts and a tight black tee shirt. He looked smaller out of his Captain's whites. Like a gym teacher. Sam pictured him with a whistle in his mouth.

There hadn't been any sand on the beach, just pebbles, small and warm, digging in through the ship's thin towels. *So many different shapes,* Sam thought. She spotted Ronnie's interest in them. The ocean was a startling shade of aquamarine, like a crayon color, and when they left his back was sunburned.

"You make me—lighter," he said in the taxi. "I love feeling

that way with you." It was the first time he'd applied the word to her. Love.

"I love you too," she said.

He pulled her to his chest and she couldn't see his face.

Olena adjusts her suit, says something in Russian. She leaves her wadded paper towels in the sink and gives Sam a half-hearted wave, revealing a tuft of armpit hair.

"What's your friend's name?" says Sam. She has an urge to hug this woman, bond with her further in a way that will give Ronnie pause.

"Larissa," says Olena, and grins like happy, faithful people do.

•   •   •   •

Sam and Ronnie's previous day off together was in Barcelona, a day usually spent at Planet Hollywood with Nacho Salads and Long Island Iced Teas. Instead, Ronnie announced he was going to buy a new fishing rod. He'd be gone all afternoon—she didn't mind, did she? They'd have their Long Island Iced Teas next week, promise.

She was surprised how little she did mind. She stayed onboard and took inventory for the costumes in the girls' dressing room, a Dance Captain duty. She had a key and locked herself in and was comforted by the lingering smells of sweat and hair spray. The feather boas dangled. She hadn't been alone in weeks.

She filled in the list.

ITEM	QUANTITY	CONDITION
Purple satin cancan dresses	6	Fair
Cowboy hats	6	Poor
Red satin cowboy shirts with fringe	4	Fair
Poodle skirts	6	Good
Feather boas	7	Fair
Yellow leotards with sequins	6	Good
Wigs, various	10	Poor

Amphibians

There were empty water bottles on the floor, and tissues blotted with lip-marks. There were barrettes and elastic bands scattered on the countertop, sticky and trailing long strands of hair.

A plan: She'd divide the counter space into two-foot sections. She'd use a roll of black electrical tape and a ruler from the Purser's desk. She'd make nametags and laminate them in the Print Room. In the prop closet she'd find the yellow plastic buckets from the axed "Singing in the Rain" routine, enough for everyone to store their make-up and fishnets.

By the time Ronnie returned from the tackle shop, the counter was sectioned with thick black lines. Sam crouched on the floor, wiping out the buckets with a damp cloth. She hummed to herself, a Carole King song she'd liked in junior high.

He made his voice low and bossy, a cartoon version of himself. "Hey there." His forehead was shiny, his armpits stained. He tapped his sandaled foot and Sam didn't stand up. He smelled different.

"It collapses or something?" The pole was navy blue to match the tackle box.

"It's telescopic." He didn't demonstrate.

Later that night, after two gin and tonics in the crew bar, Sam told Ronnie she'd left something in the dressing room. He was talking to the Staff Captain with one hand still on Sam's thigh. She'd see him back in his suite, she whispered.

She slipped up the stairs to Main Deck and unlocked the girls' side. She smoothed a wrinkle in the tape between 'Tina' and 'Gayle.' Was it one of them? She let herself cry for a minute—*It's the gin*, she'd say, if he asked—then she borrowed Gayle's cold cream and wiped away the black smudges. On the floor she counted nine sequins, one red feather and three stray bobby pins she'd missed.

Fishing

•　　　•　　　•　　　•

The line jerks. It's Ronnie's first bite of the day. "You bastard!" he says. The fish is small and shiny and flapping above the shallow waves. He drops it on the sand to wriggle for air.

"It's so tiny," says Sam, having given up on her foot. "Did you get a fishing badge too?"

He ignores this. "It's a herring."

Sam stoops down to touch it, surprised by the scales, how colorful they seem up close.

"Could we eat it?" she asks. And then she remembers. *Of course not. All that oil.*

She could nudge it back into the sea.

Sam checks to see if Olena is watching, but she's lighting a cigarette for her companion, Larissa, shielding the slight breeze with her palm. She's laughing at something Larissa has said.

Options, Sam thinks. She could get a taxi back by herself. She could move back in with Pru. She could retrieve her vanity case and her uniform and when she sees Ronnie at life boat drill and Captain's Ball and in the narrow Main Deck corridor they both pass through a dozen times a day, she'll pretend he's just a passenger dressed in white, stripes on his shoulders.

She could become angrier, sturdier. Harder to dig out.

"I'm going back now," she says. None of them look up—not the Russians, not Ronnie, who's fiddling with his line, absorbed.

"Now? Give me ten minutes," he says.

In the cab he rests his hand on Sam's crotch. "I know this great little place," he whispers, "not far from here."

It's the same bit. The cab driver watches them in the rearview mirror. Sam looks out the window so neither one of them can read her face.

"It's cozy. Secluded. Plenty of life-vests, in case of an emergency." He presses his hand down. "Or, room service," he says. "Linguine with squid and a nice bottle of Chardonnay."

"Ronnie." The cabbie looks away.

"Mm?"

"You said her rear was like a melon. Like melons."

"Yes. Honeydew."

"It's dumb, don't you think? To compare a body part to a piece of fruit?"

"What if I say I want to show you my banana?"

"It's rude."

"I'd like to get rude with you."

"Stop it," she says.

The cab driver's eyes flick back to them. Ronnie removes his hand. The cranes are frozen. Cargo containers stacked like metal Legos, red and blue boxes the size of vans.

They're quiet, for a time.

"It's a ghost town, isn't it?" says Ronnie. This is his tactic. Avoid prevailing winds. Change the course.

"It's dead," says Sam. "Like us."

"Excuse me?"

Try it on. See how it fits. "What am I now, your date?"

"You want to be the wife?" His eyebrows go up as far as they can go. He means her implication is ridiculous. He means, *I already have one of those.*

While he's fumbling for his wallet, she slams the door, races up the gangway, nearly slipping in her sandals. Security Joe doesn't say a word.

At his suite, she stops outside the door, breathing hard. She could go to the mess, calm down, drink bad coffee. But she'd have to talk with people there, answer questions—she might be tempted to explain herself to the stewards and croupiers. The pho-togs and pursers and waitresses. Tell them who she really is.

Fishing

She opens Ronnie's door. It's cool and hushed inside, like her high school library. In the bedroom, the queen-size has been made, the towels replaced. Any other day they'd fall on the bed without speaking, sunburns chafing on clean white sheets.

Find a bag, she commands. *Put things in: book, tee shirt, uniform badge.* She doesn't carry her old cabin key, but she could find Pru in the crew mess, get her to open their door.

She waits in the air-conditioned semi-darkness of the bedroom, deciding, curtains smudging out the day. The door clicks open and she hears the jangle of the tackle box. Two muffled thuds on carpet, ice rattling.

She thinks of the Russians, still on the beach. How Olena must have paused, about to dip her pearly foot into the Civitavecchian harbor.

How Ronnie must have called, "I wouldn't if I were you."

How Olena, beaming at him, had gone ahead and stepped in it anyway.

Before and After Florence

It was chilly for June. They wore sweatshirts and boots. In Paris, Vienna and Lugano, Gaby was the follower, the listener. She followed as Mo reserved the hostel beds and deciphered the maps. She held open the plastic bag of bread and cheese as Mo dipped in her multi-ringed fingers for more.

But in Florence, Gaby took over. She walked ahead. Her heels, blistered since Paris, had at last scabbed over and hardened. She heaved the heavier backpack along the Arno, slouching and turtle-necked, because the Aunt belonged to her.

The Aunt had blue on her fingers and an orange streak like a question mark on her forearm. The dusky sky behind her was almost the same shade.

"My art school," the Aunt said, rising quickly from her squat, nodding to the gray building behind her. Her earrings were complicated and shiny. She hugged them both, smelling like warm dough and limes.

"She's Italian now?" Mo asked, when the Aunt went in to get her things. "A citizen?"

"She's American," said Gaby, studying a turret. "She fucks Italians."

Then they followed the Aunt back to her apartment, the light fading quickly, the streets like the E.M. Forster movies Gaby had been forced to watch with her mother.

"I have wine," said the Aunt. "You drink?" She was looking at Mo. Her lips were neat and pouty.

"We drink," said Gaby.

●　　　●　　　●　　　●

The candelabra was her favorite, Gaby decided, gold but mottled green in places, supporting fine, finger-thin candles. "*Bahrook, a toy, add an oy,*" said the Aunt, and asked Gaby to light them all. Hanukkah in June, which the Aunt thought was funny. She wasn't Jewish, but she knew Gaby was. So much in the apartment was flammable—the gauze curtains, the bamboo blinds, the blood-colored cushions. Only the mantel looked sturdy, the row of thick silver frames containing the Aunt at a potter's wheel, the Aunt eating lobster in a plastic bib, the Aunt naked beside a short, anemic waterfall. Her breasts were pale as she arched inside the square.

"Hot," said Mo, looking, when the Aunt went to the kitchen.

"She's my Aunt," said Gaby.

"She's not your real aunt."

No, but she was related, somehow. The daughter of a cousin from her father's side. The point being, they could crash there. There was a connection.

By 3:00 am, the bottles were empty and Gaby and Mo had crammed themselves into the sofa bed. Just before dawn, Mo slung a loose arm around Gaby's waist and said, "Mickey?" Her brother's name.

●　　　●　　　●　　　●

On day two, the Aunt's boyfriend appeared, with orange spiky hair. He skimmed over the girls' straight teeth and sporty backpacks. He gripped the stem of the chipped goblet Gaby had used the night before and drank several glasses of seltzer with lime. He was a sculptor from Frankfurt, he said. He'd met the Aunt in drawing class.

When they finished their late lunch of olives and cheese, they walked in pairs to the Duomo before it closed. They bought *gelati* and took pictures. The Aunt and the boyfriend traded cones.

"I thought you said she dates Italians," said Mo.

"I didn't say *dates*," said Gaby. "Want some?" It was hazelnut.

"No," said Mo, and didn't offer her own.

●　　　●　　　●　　　●

Gaby woke to sounds of distant scraping—something hard carving into something harder. She saw the stoop, the balcony, the potted plants, the boyfriend, who ate from a blue ceramic bowl with a metal spoon. The food was steaming, whatever it was, and the cold sun was shining down on his bare, lean back. Beyond him the light was streaking down, holy looking. The sliding glass door was open, just a little, just enough to feel the air and to see the edges of potted ferns, the oversized jars of herbs on a narrow ledge.

Maybe the Aunt would paint him later, thought Gaby. Maybe she'd call it *Man, Bowl, Stoop.*

Then the boyfriend slid the door shut with a solid *whap*.

In the afternoon, they waited in line to see the David.

Mo bought a stack of expensive postcards and left them on the gift shop counter. Gaby bought a notebook with soft, handmade pages, bits of twigs and leaves blended in. Later the bits would get in the way, stopping Gaby's pen when she didn't want it to. But in the shop the notebook seemed right—a pretty, useful thing.

For her mother she bought a long, gauzy scarf with flecks of bright purple, like the CSNY album cover, the one with neon alien pods rising over a mountain, "where the eagle flies with the dove." In her mother's version of Europe, hitchhiking and miniskirts were popular. Her mother still had the skirt, brown suede with fringe, which she'd pressed under the weight of hostel mattresses to iron, a trick Gaby hadn't tried yet. She hadn't brought a skirt. In her mother's Italy there were handsome men in pairs because her mother brought a college friend too. They'd spent an extra week in Rome and missed Scandinavia completely.

In the evening, after the David, Gaby washed the coffee cups, the blue bowl, the spoon. (It was her turn, Mo reminded her.) She scraped a dried couscous grain with her fingernail and placed it carefully on her tongue.

•   •   •   •

On the evening of day four, the Aunt's friends arrived with wine bottles until the apartment was stuffed with Italian men. They smiled for the American girls. They drank. Gaby watched the boyfriend rest his free hand high on the Aunt's slim thigh.

Then the Aunt got up to heat a pot of spicy, meat-filled tortellini (from a fancy package) with two kinds of sauce, pesto and red, and they sat on her floor in a cushioned circle, some with goblets, some with blue ceramic coffee cups. The candles tilted. The Aunt's arm flapped in the air as she tried to describe her paintings. Mo took a photo with the Aunt's old-fashioned Polaroid and the flash burned in.

In the picture, which Gaby would keep in her useless, twiggy journal, she sat cross-legged and straight-backed in jeans and a red flannel shirt from L.L. Bean. Her hair was tangled and her chin was high, a sauce-stained plate at her feet. She was talking to Giorgio, who hadn't eaten all his pasta, who wore black jeans, his long legs crammed under. His shoes were made of creamy leather, which Gaby had an urge to nibble. She would taste licorice, she decided. She'd had a lot of wine by then. She bobbed her head as Giorgio stuttered over English verbs and smoked a brand of cigarettes she hadn't heard of. He didn't offer her one. His eyes darted. When the Aunt, braless, leaned over to pour more Chianti, he looked at what was under her blouse.

Later, between the ferns and spices on the balcony, Gaby let Giorgio hold onto her own breasts for a while. The kiss that followed was brief. Gaby was thinking of the shiny purple shade inside a mussel shell—what was the color exactly? Then she bit him a little on the lip.

In her journal version, she would bite harder, maybe enough to draw blood. She would not think of mussels.

•   •   •   •

In the morning, once they'd packed, the Aunt gave them focaccia bread wrapped in a pretty yellow cloth and a bottle of red. Her lips were chapped and her breath smelled sour. She kissed them goodbye, cold-looking in her sheer white slip.

"Thank you," said Mo. "I love the pictures of you."

"Thank you," said the Aunt. She looked behind at the sleeping boyfriend, who didn't get up to see them off.

"We'll call when we get there," said Gaby, who wouldn't call the Aunt for years, who'd leave the yellow cloth on a station bench even though Mo had specifically said she wanted to keep it as a souvenir.

•   •   •   •

On the train to Madrid, Mo made Gaby sit close so hairy German men wouldn't touch her.

"What German men?" said Gaby.

Gaby's fingers were cramped from writing. She stopped writing and watched everything rush by beautifully through the grubby glass of the train. She thought about the waterfall.

• • • •

Back in Maine, Gaby's mother said, "Does it look the same? I still haven't seen your pictures."

"I don't know," said Gaby. They had a DVD to watch later. They were drinking rosé. The coldness outside seeped in through the old, worn boards. "It's the same, yes. The Duomo, the David. We had *gelati*."

In the photograph, the goblets are full and the plates are soiled. Someone's wooly socks are blue. A stranger's hand flaps at the edge, cut off at the wrist.

"You were right," Gaby added, guilty. "The light was perfect there."

If you caught it in time, she meant. The light in Florence could make plain gray stone into something brilliant and warm.

Good Neighbors

It's foggy. You've known him since you were fourteen and your sturdy clothing touches his sturdy clothing. You sit where you sat last year, port side on top. You hear the same stories from the Captain's loudspeaker voice about the milky nubs of land you should know by now.

This is the trip that will decide things, you decide. There is a roiling like tides in your gut because he doesn't kiss you any-more. Because you don't kiss him. Although you're still sitting together on the top deck.

You dock. You lug your bags from the pier, up the hill, down the road to Crab Beach and you feel your heart thumping as he walks ahead. You have to stop four times. Trucks go by with luggage piled up and you wonder if the drivers think you're foolish or tough for walking it.

You climb the stairs to the rental and hope he kicked the dirt from his boots before he opened the door. You put your underwear in one drawer and your t-shirts in another. You call your parents and say you've arrived. You eat grapes and no longer feel seasick. You make him a turkey and cheese sandwich with mustard because you forgot to pack the mayo. You sprinkle Smartfood on the side.

You watch him eat. You take the porch chair with the moldy cushion and start to read the *New York Times Book Review* but soon you notice the ducks and boys and buoys, which reminds you of bathroom signs in seafood restaurants: Buoys and Gulls. The boys on the beach are fatter this year. They don't wave and you don't wave. They're shirtless and yelling about the rowboat.

When you finish the *Book Review* you can start the novel you brought. When you read the novel you brought, you can read the books left behind by other guests. One is *The Beans of Egypt, Maine*, which, you're ashamed to say, you've never read. You want to be more of a Mainer this week. You promise, as you did last year, to buy a very good map and memorize where you are.

You read the new messages in the guestbook. The week before, someone wrote, "Luke will be back—I'm sure of it." You think of *Star Wars* and then remember that Luke is the landlady's son, a shouter, a torturer of island cats. You think the message means he's probably not coming back this year. You hope that's the case.

As the fog fades you begin to see the smaller island across the tiny harbor, called Smutty Nose. You see day-trippers sitting at picnic tables with lobster bibs. The market must be open.

"The market must be open," you say. He nods and eats his Smartfood.

You go to the market, where the landlady works behind the register, one of two other jobs she has on the island besides being the landlady. You hug the landlady and she smells nice, like soap and lemons. Not at all like fish. You ask about Luke and she says, "He's a good kid." They're out of crab rolls, which disappoints you more than it should. You try to hide your disappointment from the landlady. They do have scallops, shrimp and tuna, she says. And lobsters of course, but you know he likes to save lobsters for the last night.

Amphibians

You go back to the porch. "Lobster rolls are $12.50," you say. He doesn't say anything. You go back and order the fish chowder in a firm paper cup.

On the porch you burn your tongue but you keep on eating. The sun is brighter now and you sweat and wish you hadn't chosen something so hot to put in your mouth.

You make hot tea. You drink tea and feel it on your burned tongue. You feel guilty and make a cup for him too.

You read.

You get up and look at the shelf and find a book called *Along the Maine Coast* from 1967. The pictures look like 1967, the people dusty and wide-collared. You note that this is the year your parents met.

On a legal pad, you copy, "Gloomy thoughts of long-past massacres, hunger, war—of which this region had its ample share—seem out of place." The syntax is weird but you keep copying because the sentence is about the place where you were born. You also copy, "The prevailing southwest winds bring sparkling days to the area" and "This region is often called the boating capital of New England."

You wonder if it's still called this. You look at more pictures of shipyards and remember that in your Valedictorian speech you said, "If building a skiff makes you happy, build a skiff." You wish you hadn't said this. You asked your father for the right word. *Not vessel,* he'd said. *Try skiff.* You wonder if your father thought it was a dumb thing to say altogether.

Your parents paid for the week on the island, even though you have a decent job at a college in New Jersey. "Her parents are both lawyers in town," the boat ticket-taker had said to the Captain, just before you boarded. This was the ticket-taker's way of introducing you to the Captain, who was standing by the space heater in the ticket booth to keep warm. He didn't wear a Captain's hat. You were carrying the *Times* when you met him. Your mother had just settled the ticket taker's divorce.

•   •   •   •

After teatime, you suggest a walk. He agrees. He puts on the expensive North Face boots you bought him for his birthday. You hike to the large rusted anchor and then to Hendricks Head. You sweat. You feel tired and healthy. You lose sight of him twice, three times. The third time you say, "Hello?" because there's a choice, right or left. You choose right and there he is, looking out at the soupy sea alone. From the ledge where, twenty years ago, three island children slipped and drowned. A small sign says so.

"You didn't hear me?" you say.

The next time he stops for a drink of water, you make a sound like a seal and ask if he remembered to bring the Scrabble board. He nods. You walk again.

Back in town, you stop at the store with the yellow sign where the locals have benched in for beer. The cashier doesn't look up. She's trying to find something in a ratty encyclopedia. You shift the gallon of water from one arm to the other.

"Joseph Conrad," says the cashier when she finds it.

A man with suspenders, the owner, nods as though a bet is at stake.

There's only one book for sale in the store and it's by the owner's wife—you remember it from last year. It won a poetry prize and there's a gold sticker on every copy to prove it.

You buy orange juice from the other grocery store while he heads back to the porch to read. You don't have to ask him to carry the water jug.

•   •   •   •

On the porch you notice the musty Saltine smell your sweat makes. You want to take a shower but the landlady, who lives right below, might think it's odd to shower in the evening.

Amphibians

You don't want her to think you're a water waster. You want to be naked and clean, though. You eat tortilla chips and salsa on the deck and hold your book in your lap. He's reading *The Brethren,* which is about the Supreme Court. He hasn't told you much about the book but last week, when you were staying at your parents' house, your mother asked him about it and he replied in more detail.

He puts on his hiking boots again and this is how you know he's going to the market before it closes. Still, you ask, "Are you going to buy fish?"

He nods.

You put on your orange Crocs, which you only wear in Maine, and follow him out.

He decides on scallops. He makes scallops. You offer to help and he shakes his head and later you offer again and he lets you peel potatoes.

You eat scallops in garlic and rosemary with mashed potatoes and a small salad because produce is so expensive on the island. It's all very good and you tell him so.

You have a glass of Oxford Landing with your meal. He looks out the window in the direction of Smutty Nose but it's too dark to see. You listen to the sound of lapping waves through the screen. It feels foggy again and the dampness curls in. When he's done he clears his plate. You finish eating. You wait until your stomach feels not so full and then clear your own plate. You do all the dishes. You let them dry.

"Thanks for washing up," he says, not looking at you. You wonder if he wants to see you naked. You're not naked now but you wonder if you'll be naked later. Why wouldn't he want to see you naked? You sit down to read. You thank him for dinner. He nods.

You put out chocolate cookies and tea. You say, "What type of fish could be cooked in red wine?" He doesn't know. He takes out his crosswords.

You wonder if you should go to bed. Then you read some more. Then you say, "I think I'm going to bed." He nods. When you kiss him on the cheek, he doesn't turn away. His lips twitch a little. They are very pretty lips. You don't tell him this. And then you go to bed.

Inside it's a ghost room and you're sure there are short, dead soldiers trapped in the walls. Your skin is not clean and you worry about your crevices. You calculate how long your body has been away from soapy water. You start to hate the bed, the heavy covers, the soldiers lurking. You wonder about your parents—whether they're talking to each other or reading right now.

You get up and trip on your suitcase. You swear. Maybe he'll hear you and ask how you are. The ghosts are quiet but the door creaks when you push it open and he looks up at you and then down at his book. You see that he has opened another beer. You scrub yourself with a washcloth but it's not the same.

When you come back he's in bed and the clock has been turned toward the wall. His hands are folded on his stomach like a vampire. You keep your eyes open and don't reach for him. He doesn't reach for you.

In the morning you will shower first thing.

●　　　●　　　●　　　●

In the morning you can't remember the coffee ratio from last year. It's an odd-shaped pot, larger than the one in your apartment. *I took a guess*, you'll tell him, if the coffee turns out wrong. From the porch you can see a little girl swimming and some grown-ups watching her. You watch the girl too and then you read the novel you brought, which is about a Midwestern woman who just moved to New York City. She sleeps on the floor of her studio apartment until her futon arrives. Everything is just about to happen for her.

Amphibians

From the bathroom window you can see the landlady hanging her clothes out to dry. "Sure—Luke would like that," she says to her neighbor. And then, "That was a long haul."

The neighbor doesn't say anything for a while. Then they talk about video games, their sons' favorites.

The landlady says she would have liked them too, at that age. "That's all he does," she says.

The neighbor says Luke should bring his own sleeping bag. Then they talk about the librarian's collection of geodes.

You stay in the shower for a very long time. You drink coffee and eat Cheerios. You do yoga stretches and then return to the porch. There are ducks on the beach, and the little girl isn't swimming anymore.

You think the bookstore will be open soon.

You try to sketch the rocking chair in front of the neighbor's house, which has fishing line crisscrossed at the back. It looks like it couldn't hold the weight of the neighbor or the neighbor's son. You compose a theory about body types. Better to be large and rugged, ready to row a boat, lift bait barrels, teach your boy to fish when your husband leaves or drowns.

You remember what your father said, of your luggage. *You going to be able to lift that?*

You write on your bookmark, "If we could switch bodies, would we like each other more?" You rip the bookmark into many pieces and put the pieces in your pocket. You need a new bookmark now.

You make a list on a napkin and call it, *Places I Have Heard Seagulls:*

1) New York City
2) Agadir, Morocco
3) Barcelona, Spain
4) Brighton, England
5) Maine

Good Neighbors

It doesn't seem possible that you've actually been to the middle places. You don't talk about them anymore because you went there with someone else. He's been to a lot of places too, with his ex, and you don't ask him about those places either.

You cram the napkin between your legs when you hear him close the bathroom door.

He's on the couch in his pajamas, reading. His face is tired and pretty. He's drinking tea from the largest cup he can find. He left the seat up, which you decide isn't necessarily a secret message.

"I'm going to the bookstore," you say, but then decide not to, once you're walking down the dirt road in your Crocs. Instead you go to the Gift Emporium and try to look at every item in the store. You think you've caught them all. You buy a small map of Maine.

When you come back he doesn't ask about the bookstore so you don't have to lie about where you've been, even though you're looking at the new map of Maine. You have a crab roll for lunch and can't finish the doughy bun. He asks if you're going to finish it.

"No," you say. "Do you want it?"

"No," he says. "It's just dough." Then you put it in the compost pail.

•   •   •   •

You hike together on a different trail, and it's good to sweat and move the air around your chest. You make a list of three things you want to write down and go over the list in loops. You mustn't forget. (You don't think 'mustn't' at the time but you intend to write it down this way.) You watch the ground because there's so much to trip over—roots and rocks and old gray boards with rusted rods sliced through. Dock pilings? He's up ahead, just beyond the thorny row of bushes. You pick up your pace and listen for the swish of his windbreaker—but it's just the swish of you, your own windbreaker. "Hello?" you say, and there's nothing.

The path goes into woods or along water. You choose woods and you know as you take it it's wrong but you don't stop. *This will show how plucky I am.* He'll take the trail all the way around the perimeter because he likes the water trails best. Not a big deal. You'll cross somewhere or he'll wait for you on a bluff.

But the next small green trail sign on the rock ledge doesn't seem to point anywhere. *There should be better arrows*, you think. The ledge is steep and everything is grown over with dry twiggy branches, waist-high. They scratch and pull at you, biting at the tight netting in your backpack where the water bottle goes, making a hole. "Fuck," you say. You think of the stories of lost boys in Maine, always boys, and how the sign at the island dock said, *Don't hike alone. Tell someone where you're going.* You remember the lost boy on Mt. Katahdin from the book your 4th grade teacher read aloud, a true story. The boy found a gunnysack to sleep in but there was a mouse already living inside. It scurried out and Jimmy Grinnan had interrupted to ask if the mouse would die. You'd been wondering about that too.

Survival of the fittest, the teacher had said, meaning, tough luck for the mouse. It was a clear answer and Jimmy was quiet then.

You're not fit—you're watching yourself from above and it looks like you're panicking. A twisted ankle or a tumble down the rocks—it could happen.

You decide to turn around. You don't have to walk the perimeter. You can just go back to the porch and wait. You have *The Beans of Egypt, Maine* to get through.

You're not quitting; you're just being smart. No need for both of you to be hiking alone. You're following the rules of hiking.

Good Neighbors

You have the sun block and bug spray in your backpack and you wonder if he'll need them. You remember that you have a cell phone. You wonder if he'll borrow someone's cell phone in town and call yours to make sure you're okay.

You remember a line from a British comedy series you own on DVD—the office boss who says, "Her own decisions!" of the one female employee. But it's only distracting for a small moment and then you start to cry. Why didn't you tell anyone where you were going? You decide that's how you'll begin when you see him again. "We didn't confer." And then you'll make a joke about *Winnie the Pooh*. Tigger circling and circling and ending up at the same spot.

It's a cliché, he might say.

But it's true, you think.

Your face is wet. You get a tissue out and use it. You smell the tissue but it only smells like tissue.

If you ask him to slow down next time, he'll say, "I'm walking as slowly as I can." He'll use the adverb, slowly. He'll say you took the wrong path and you'll believe him because it was nice not to follow, nice to stop and think, until you began to panic.

You wonder if *What happened?* is a better way to start. He says you're too aggressive sometimes. What about, *You did the same thing yesterday. Can't you look behind to see if I'm still there?* Should you even speak first? He won't speak and won't speak and you could say, *Isn't this dumb, to waste the week we look forward to all year long?* But that implies blame and you shouldn't do that.

What if you see him now? Will your face look right?

You won't see him. He isn't on this trail. So you take your time. You sit twice, three times along the way—flat ground, easy path. Pleasing ass-shaped rocks. Same dry twigs and sharp ledges. Driftwood with nails. You see exactly where you are now. You feel better. You don't have to rush because he's walking the perimeter.

Amphibians

In town you go to the art gallery and then the ice cream place. You order chocolate almond frozen yogurt and decide to eat it all instead of saving some in the freezer for him. You're holding the cup as you trudge up the steps.

And there he is, on the porch, which surprises you. You wonder if your face looks right. He isn't consuming anything. He's reading and waiting with his expensive sunglasses on.

You think, *Is it wrong to be eating ice cream?*

"What happened?" you say. Your tone may not be right. The ice cream is good and you keep eating it. You sit down and squint. He's smiling for the first time since you've arrived on the island.

"I don't know. What happened?" He went to Puffin Point, he said. He waited for a while.

"You lost me," you say.

"It wasn't hard."

"You seem concerned," you say.

"I was concerned. You could have called 9-1-1."

It's funny, he means. You were alone on the trail and it's funny. You keep eating. "Maybe you can walk slowly next time," you say.

"Maybe you can walk faster."

"I'm walking as fast as I can."

You sound pathetic.

But the silence is done. He's your friend again and it's so tiring anyway, staying steely with him. The ghosts turn away. Your ice cream is delicious. You offer him some. He doesn't want any and he doesn't care that you're having dessert before dinner.

You take a second shower and change. You have a glass of wine, and another. The steeliness doesn't fade completely. It rises again, a different form. But you read together on the porch. You make dinner plans. Shrimp in garlic and butter;

mac and cheese with tomatoes and cucumbers. He cooks again and you do the dishes. He has ice cream just before the shop closes. He tells you about the book he's reading.

When the sun sets, golds and pinks you want to save on your phone, you stay outside even when you need a sweater. He stays inside reading. The wind makes the fog fade and the night sky clears. Under the moon, the dinghy rocks in the dark and that's how you know the tide's coming in. You hear the creak of the small boat budging over and over on the sand. But it's roped to something, tied up earlier by the neighbor's boy.

You move before your brain can catch up, down the steps and towards the sound. Wet sand on wool socks, cold seeping through. (How delicious the change in sensation.) You touch the rod, the hook, the loose knot. Your fingers are fast, like you've done this before.

Sudden lights from the neighbor's house. A voice saying, "You!" But it's already done. The dinghy heaves and bobs, pushing itself away, trailing the rope behind.

Acknowledgements

Thank you to all at Leapfrog Press for allowing this collection to swim. Thanks to Ramona Ausubel for seeing it clearly. Special thanks to Lisa Graziano, Ann Weinstock and Rebecca Cuthbert for your commitment and vision.

Thanks to my incredible agent, Stacia Decker, who's had my back for years.

Thanks to Mary Bisbee-Beek for publicity insights and encouragement.

Thanks to Tantor Media for audiobook expertise.

Thanks to my brilliant teachers: Jeremy Gavron, Judith Grossman, CJ Hribal, Bill Roorbach, Jim Shepard, Joan Silber and Peter Turchi.

Thank you for your generous words, Cynthia Brackett-Vincent, Porter Fox and Joan Silber.

Thanks to The Mullen Education Center in Becket, MA, for my sweet office space.

Thank you to the following magazines and literary organizations who published* and/or awarded versions of the stories collected here:

Schaffner Press (*Amphibians*, runner-up, Nicholas Schaffner Award for Music in Literature, 2019)
Hidden River Arts (*Amphibians*, finalist, Hawk Mountain Collection Award, 2019)
*Nowhere Magazine ("Amphibians," Finalist, Spring Award, 2017; Pushcart Prize nominee, 2017)
*10th Anniversary Nowhere Print Annual, 2018 ("Amphibians")
*nidus, 2004 ("Dishdash")